Everyday Angels

by John Tunnell

Contents

1 The Game 4

2 Real Life? 19

3 Which Path? 33

4 Better than I Thought 44

5 Choices, Choices 54

6 That Seems Odd 69

7 The Truth 80

8 Commentary 89

9 Let's Review 101

10 The Impact 117

11 Reflections 130

12 Make it Right 142

13 Let The Trials Begin 150

14 The End of the Road 167

1 The Game

Matthew Jacobs is a quiet man who lives behind the scenes. He doesn't believe himself to be anything or anyone special. He never walks towards the limelight. It is actually invisible to him. He supports those who seek fame and fortune, but has no interest in it for himself. His job is to provide tech support for celebrities and CEOs for live shows. He wears all black most of the time so he can't be seen backstage. He is there to work and never get any credit for it. Nobody knows his name. He is basically anonymous and unseen. He is paid enough to keep his interest. He doesn't really want for anything, except a deeper meaning to his life.

He has always felt like there was more. In his soul he felt a longing, a calling if you will that he felt he was not living up to. He has no real family to speak of. It wouldn't really matter if he did. He is never home anyway. His work takes him all over the world. Every day is a new city, a new hotel, a new crew, and a new set of trials. His life has been in flux for many years now.

As a younger man he had worked near home. He saw his family every day. He loved them and was loved. But now that life seems foreign to him. It just feels like one long string of never-ending tasks for ungrateful people that become increasingly more demanding with each passing year. He has lots of shallow relationships with acquaintances all over the world, but very few real friendships.

He has a deep loneliness that he has to keep covered up to protect himself. But by covering it up he makes the problem worse. There is a part of him that feels hopeless. He wants to feel like he matters. He wants to be loved. He wants to be a part of something bigger than himself, but he knows he has to keep doing what he is doing for many more years before anything will change. He has tried to get out of the business for years but his phone continues to ring and the money is hard to turn down.

There is almost no joy in his career any more. He got into this line of work by accident and hasn't been able to find a way out. No one ever dreams of sitting back stage in the dark and getting yelled at when they are a kid. He fears that eventually one of two things will happen. Either he will die on show site while working or he will die alone and no one will even notice he is dead until someone reports the smell. Either way he will be alone. He fears he will die as he has lived, someone of very little importance that won't be missed when he is gone.

When he is off the clock he fills his time with tasks that kept his mind too busy to notice how bad his life has become. He is always in the middle of several important sounding projects. From the outside it would be easy to assume that he has it all. But in reality there is a battle constantly raging inside of him that feels like it is ripping him apart.

Lately, and he doesn't know why, he feels like every part of him is under a microscope constantly. He feels strangers judging him. And in reality they are. Just not the way he thinks. Like most of us, his life is largely illusion and misperception. He is in show business and yet doesn't fully realize how important he is to the show. In fact, without him there would be no show at all.

Speaking of shows, he does all types of shows. Medical conventions, sales meetings, corporate rallies, concerts, music videos, live television, sports, news, movies, TV shows, church events, politics, charities, cartoons, product launches and much more. He never knows exactly what he is doing until he shows up at the location. He is simply given dates, a location, and a day rate. Apart from that he knows very little. Over the years he has become very versatile with his skillset. He remains calm in stressful situations. He adapts easily. And for this very reason he is in high demand.

When the show is over it is over for him. He sends an invoice and forgets about it. He doesn't waste time or energy reliving the minutia of any given show or how it could have gone differently. He has no real vested interest in anything he does. He wants it to go well, but at the end of the day he doesn't really care one way or the other. It seems like unimportant fluff that is of no real consequence to him. There have only been a handful of shows he has done in his whole career that made any kind of impact on his life. Unfortunately the mundane outweighs the inspirational most of the time.

Recently Matthew took a show in his hometown. It didn't pay much, but a friend begged him to do it. He had the dates open on his calendar and so he agreed. He had a pretty firm policy of not working for cheap or free because he felt like it hurt the industry when freelancers did that. On this particular show he felt compelled. All the planets seemed to align and all signs pointed towards doing the show. It was easy and smooth. No snags. No stress. No irritating clients. The crew was fun. They had good catering. It was everything he always wanted in a show if he was being honest.

And it was a faith-based event. He felt that he needed some more God in his life. He hadn't really noticed until now but there was a moral drift that he had been experiencing. It was one that upon further reflection he had allowed through his choices and lack of discipline, as we often do.

The show started with the usual niceties and introductions. After a few minutes they went into a group activity. These usually attempt to bond strangers by forcing them to work together as a team. What it meant for Matthew was a relaxed hour with very little cues. He could simply switch cameras back and forth every once and a while. He could talk on headset with the rest of the crew. He could update his Facebook status. He could disengage from the show and not get yelled at. Typically when these types of things would happen he would take the first few minutes to get familiar with the bit and then once he saw the pattern he could settle into doing basically nothing.

This presenter was different though. He was a charismatic man who seemed very comfortable on stage. He didn't read from a teleprompter or lean heavily on his power point presentation. He knew his material. He believed what he said. He spoke with conviction. The crowd was engaged and honestly so was Matthew. Crew chatter ceased immediately. The presenter commanded the audience. He started by asking the audience to list ten bad things that could happen to them. As people answered he would write each bad thing on a separate piece of paper.

1) Develop an addiction
2) Overdose and die from said addiction
3) Get fat
4) Get mugged
5) Be alone forever
6) Go bankrupt
7) Get an STD
8) Watch someone die
9) Commit suicide
10)   Start World War 3

He then asked the audience to list ten good things that could happen to them. Ironically, the bad list was much easier to come up with than the good list. Matthew saw the audience struggle to come up with ten good things that could happen to them. The first few were easy, but it was like nobody had ever thought about more than three good things ever happening to them. Eventually they got ten.

1) Learn a new trade that you love
2) Be healthy
3) Be physically fit
4) Find the love of your life

5) Defeat your demons
6) Live at peace
7) Be healed from a long term ailment
8) Experience true freedom
9) Change the world for the better
10)   Win the lottery

Zeke, the presenter, wrote each of the good things on separate pieces of paper as he had done with the bad things. He asked for a volunteer. He chose someone out of the sea of hands. He then stepped off the stage and went to the front of the audience. He pulled out a blindfold and put it on the volunteer who's name was Paul. He made sure Paul couldn't see anything. He laid all the pieces of paper out in front of Paul in a path. He explained as he did that the man could easily walk this path with his eyes open. He could step on every good thing and avoid every bad thing effortlessly if he could only see the path laid out before him. But it would be very difficult to do that now that he was blindfolded. He asked the audience if anyone would be willing to help this man.

Hands went up everywhere. He chose someone from the far side of the room. He asked the person if he knew Paul. He didn't. He looked very seriously at the second volunteer and said, "Now you have become Paul's conscience. Your fate is tied to his. Wherever he lands, whatever piece of paper he steps on will now happen to both of you. You cannot touch him. You cannot force him. You can only talk at a reasonable level next to him. You will not have a microphone. He must walk the whole path. There is no turning back from this point forward. Do you think you can do that?"

The second volunteer whose name was Noah replies, "That is so easy, of course. It is a simple path. You can easily do this Paul. We've got this." He looks at the presenter and says, "What do we get if we win?" The presenter laughs, "I already told you. You get the rewards or consequences on the pieces of paper. These will really happen to you. Choose your steps carefully." Noah laughs uncomfortably. "Do you still think this is easy?" the presenter asks. "Slightly less now" Noah nervously answers. "Well, we have a few more twists" the presenter says, "Now I need to ask the audience for one more list. List ten good deeds that a person can do." The audience is fully engaged at this point and so is Matthew. They make the list:

1) Inspire someone who has lost hope
2) Help an enemy
3) Give away something that is precious to you
4) Turn the other cheek
5) Love the unlovely
6) Be a friend to someone who desperately needs your friendship
7) Volunteer and expect nothing in return
8) Forgive the one who has hurt you the worst
9) Ask forgiveness from the ones you have hurt and then do whatever it takes to make it right with them.
10)   Give away everything you have

The presenter writes each of these on separate pieces of paper as well. He then rearranges the path with the good deeds in the path. "If you step on a bad thing it will happen to you. If you step on a good thing that will happen to you as well, BUT only if you have stepped on a good deed. You can store up good deeds. It will cost you one good deed for every good thing you get but it doesn't matter what order they happen. Do you still think you can do it?" Noah, the conscience, nods his head reluctantly.

Paul, who has been blindfolded this whole time, is getting a little anxious. "Is it too late to back out? I don't do well under pressure." Matthew laughs out loud backstage, but then catches himself. The presenter smiles and says, "I'm afraid it is. Once you raised your hand you gave consent. You are committed. You have to walk the path set before you and live with the consequences of the path you choose.

So listen carefully to whatever Noah tells you Paul. Remember his fate is tied to yours. He has your best interest at heart. Oh yeah, there is one last thing before we get started. I need the rest of the audience to stand on both sides of the path. Oh yes, you are a part of this too.

Audience, your job is to misdirect Paul. You can say or do literally anything you want. There are no rules for you. You can't touch him, but you can say anything true or false. You can yell. You can use my microphone if you want. You can lie. You can tell the truth. You can act sympathetic while giving bad information. Your job is to make sure these two fail. That's it. Does everyone understand?"

The crowd seems very happy to get to participate. They start to come up with plans amongst themselves. They laugh and whisper and scheme together. The presenter says "No pressure, but this will be timed. You have 5 minutes to walk the path. If you don't make it all the way across the finish line you will lose all the good things you have accumulated and you will have to live with the consequences of all the bad things. Do you understand? Good. Your journey begins in 3,2,1. Start the clock."

Noah is shocked, "Wait! We are starting already? And there is a time limit? Ok Paul. We have to do this together. We don't have a lot of time. Lift your left foot up and move it forward about sixteen inches. No your left foot. The other left."

While Noah tries to guide Paul the crowd shouts loudly. "No the other one. Don't listen to him. Sixteen inches? Why do you want him to lose? It's more like two feet. Jump over the bad thing. Just give up and run across before the time runs out! Noah, stop trying to make him step there! Paul doesn't want to go to prison. You have to back up and jump if you don't want to lose a limb!"

Noah quickly becomes frustrated, "No. Don't listen to them. Listen to me. I am on your side. They just want to lead you astray. Left foot up. Yes like that. Move it forward about sixteen inches. Don't shift your weight yet. Keep going. Perfect. Start to put your left foot down. Yes. That's it. Put it down. Yes! You did it. You inspired someone who had lost hope. Great work. Now lift up your right foot and put it next to your left foot. There is a reward waiting for you."

The crowd never stops with the chaos. Paul hears a woman's voice over the microphone, "Look I don't want you to get hurt. Just listen to me. It's a little farther to the right than Noah is telling you. I don't think he understands how to explain what you need to do. Move your right foot about a foot directly in front of the other one. You will win the lottery." Paul swings his right foot forward quickly. He feels panicked. He is about to put it down when Noah yells "NO! Don't listen to her. Pull back a foot or you will get fat! Nobody wants that."

Paul is flustered and doesn't know who to listen to. He has already shifted his weight and his foot falls on the piece of paper that says, "Get fat". Noah sighs loudly. The crowd laughs and cheers. They high five each other. This pattern goes on for five minutes. Paul misses most of the good things on his path and steps on most of the bad things. The few good things that he does get are disqualified because he doesn't do good deeds to deserve them. In the end it doesn't matter because he gets off the path and never crosses the finish line. The crowd has led him out of the room and down the hallway but convinced him he is landing on good things despite what Noah keeps telling him.

Matthew is engrossed in this whole concept. He has a camera follow the action everywhere so that he can watch it all unfold. The presenter then removes the blindfold and shows Paul where he is. Paul was completely lost and confused. What he thought was the right path was about fifty feet away from any part of the path at all. He walks over to where the actual path is and shakes his head. "That should have been so easy. It is literally twenty feet long. Two thirds of these things are good. How did I get so lost so fast?" Noah is exasperated, "I was telling you exactly what to do. Why didn't you just listen to me? This should have been so easy, but it was so frustrating!"

The presenter puts his hands on both of their shoulders and smiles. "Fortunately for both of you there are no real consequences for the path you just walked. You can all go back to your seats now. Thank you for helping me to teach you a valuable lesson. I hope you can all apply this to your life from this point forward. The world will scream at you to do the wrong thing, but the still small voice is the one you should be listening to if you want to walk the straight and narrow path set out before you. The hard road ends up being the easiest road if you follow your conscience. Never forget that."

The presenter goes on to talk about how we should obey God even if it doesn't make sense because He can see the path that we can't. All this inspires Matthew. This show went on his short list of shows that were actually enjoyable. He wasn't even going to take the gig, but he was genuinely happy he did.

Normally he never met the people who were on the stage unless they needed something from him. But this particular presenter saw Matthew from across the room and smiled. He walked over to him and introduced himself. He encouraged Matthew and told him not to lose heart. He told him how important he was. He looked him in the eyes and asked, "Do you understand how important it is to listen to the still, small voice? Do you know the gravity of the situation? Do you know how important you are?"

Matthew laughed, "I'm not important at all. I'm just a guy back stage in black. I can be replaced in a second."

"That couldn't be farther from the truth. You are the show. You....." He pauses and seems to blank out for several seconds.

Matthew humbly put his head down. "That is very kind of you to say, but we both know it isn't true."

After an awkward pause the presenter comes out of his trance, "I have said too much. I have to go now. Stay strong Matthew. Choose wisely. What you do matters. I am rooting for you."

As the presenter walks away Matthew feels like he has hope for the first time in a long time. Like he matters. He holds his head a little higher and goes back to work. He coils cables and puts gear in cases. He loads the truck and is about to leave when one of the guys on the crew asks him if he wants to get high with the rest of the guys. Matthew has been sober for many years at this point in his life. For some reason today this seemed like a good idea to him. He was compelled even though it was out of character for him.

He followed the crew out to the parking lot and one of the guys started smoking from a pipe. He passed it to the next guy who passed it to Matthew. Matthew thought for a moment. He looked at the other guys. He felt a real struggle inside of him. For some reason these drugs were calling his name that night, more like screaming his name. He shook his head and then he looked at the pipe and the lighter in his hands and he said, "I don't want to be owned by this. No thank you." He passed it to the next person who hung his head and passed it to the next guy. One by one they passed it to the next person without taking a hit. Eventually they put it away.

One of the guys speaks up, "Man, that was a pretty cool show, huh?" Someone else chimes in, "Yeah man, that was some deep stuff they were talking about too. Kind of makes you rethink your life choices a little doesn't it?"

Matthew says, "I felt like that presenter was talking directly to me the whole time." Another guy speaks up, "Me too." The whole group agrees that they felt convicted.

Matthew breaks the silence; "I need to make some changes in my life. I have waited long enough. I think inside I have been waiting for an opportunity like this for a long time. I don't know why I needed an excuse to do the right thing. It is as if I have been waiting for permission. I am realizing we should always do the right thing. I think I am going to take a break from doing shows for a while and try to find myself. I have been coasting for a very long time. I feel lost. I need to get my priorities straight."

The youngest guy in the group says, "Don't stay gone too long old man. Someone is going to steal your seat. You might not have a place at the table when you come back hungry."

Matthew looks concerned. One of the camera ops encourages him, "Take as long as you need brother. There will always be work for you. Nothing is more important than making sure the trajectory of your life is headed in the right direction. Adjust your moral compass. Retreat to move forward. And when and if you are ready to come back this will all still be here waiting for you."

Matthew doesn't really have a plan for his life yet. He just wanders off from the crowd and starts walking to his car. It is dark and very late at night. As he unlocks his car door he hears a voice behind him. "Hey man. Stop!" He is startled and turns around. There is a middle-aged man in black running up to him. The man steps into the light. "I'm Ed. I was doing records on that show with you."

"Nice to meet you. I'm Matthew." Ed keeps talking, "I just wanted to tell you how brave that was of you back there."

Matthew is confused, "Brave? What did I do that was brave?"

"Standing up to all that peer pressure and saying no. That was a big deal man. I haven't been able to say no to drugs since I was twelve. I have struggled with addiction my whole life. I had lost hope. I didn't feel like anyone could ever actually overcome this stuff. Honestly, I was going to get really high and then go home and kill myself tonight. That was my plan.

But what that guy said in the meeting and then what you did...well, it gives me hope. I haven't had that in a really long...I don't know if I have ever really had hope. I just wanted to thank you. You saved my life."

He hugs Matthew's neck and starts to cry. Matthew is not an affectionate man. He doesn't know what to do so he just pats Ed on the back awkwardly. After a minute Ed wipes the tears away and gains his composure. "Thanks again brother. Stay strong." He walks away. He looks like a huge burden has just been lifted off his shoulders. He stands a little taller. Matthew reflects back on the day and realizes how slouched over and sad he had looked earlier in the day. Why hadn't he noticed? Why hadn't he offered to help?

Matthew gets in his car and whispers to himself, "I want to do more things like that. I want to do more things that make a difference. I had no idea that guy was suicidal. He seemed like he had it together. I never would have suspected he was suicidal. I suppose I look like I have it together too? To people who don't know any better. That couldn't be farther from the truth. I am lost. I am crumbling on the inside. I am a hollow shell of a person going through the motions in life, but not really living it. I am putting on a show for people who don't care one way or the other. I don't know what I am going to do with my life, but I am tired of living like this."

2 Real Life?

That night Matthew laid awake in bed and thought a lot about his life and the direction he wanted to go with it. He didn't really know how to do anything except production work. He had some money saved, but not enough to retire. He realized that he was exhausted. He had been working with no breaks for a very long time. He went from one gig to the next to the next. Most of the time he would double dip which meant he would be working on content for another show while he was on the current show. He could make twice as much money by doing that and he got bored easily so it kept his mind busy.

He wrestled with what he could do that would actually make a difference in the world. He tried to think of people that he knew that were inspirational or philanthropic. This was particularly difficult for him because he lived behind the curtain where he saw people for who they really were. He knew their tricks and their gimmicks and how easy it was to make monsters look like saints. After deep reflection he came up with no significant role model that he aspired to be. So he decided that he would have to pave his own path. He would pioneer a way for the people that came after him.

If he were to be honest his motivations were at least partly selfish. For years he felt empty. He felt like he walked around with a hole in his pocket. He worked hard. He made a lot of money, but it always seemed to disappear. And so did his happiness. Living your life for selfish gain and pleasure leaves a person just feeling more and more lost, alone and unfulfilled. He really just wanted to do good things so that good things would happen to him. He saw that displayed in the demonstration that night and it struck him deep in his heart. He realized that he had to do his part or things would never change.

After hours of reflection he had no clue what to do next. He dozed off. His sleep was restless. He woke up from a troubling dream and then it hit him. He couldn't see the path laid out before him because he was the one who was blindfolded. He was the one who needed help. He was waving his hands around in the darkness trying to find what someone else could easily see. But, was there really someone that could and would help him if he asked? And what would they ask for in return for this enormous favor?

Without a thought he says out loud, "If anyone can hear me, I can't see what you can see. I am lost. I need help. Please guide me on my path. I don't know where to go or what to do. I would love to have a conscience to help guide me. I don't know what you would want in return from me. I will try to do the right thing to make your job easier. I will try to listen, but I need to know your voice. Can you show me that you hear me? Can you give me some sort of a sign?"

He pauses and sits in silence for a moment. He feels a little stupid saying those things to what may be nobody at all. After about twenty anxious seconds he hears a crowd cheering outside. He tilts his head and listens. He walks up to the window and there is a parade outside. He reads some of the signs that the people are holding, but it is unclear what the parade is for. The signs talk about awareness, but had no details about what kind of awareness they are referring to.

He fully opens the blinds and stands in front of the window. He feels like the crowd is looking at him, but he doesn't try to hide from their view. Someone from the crowd makes eye contact with him and tilts their sign in his direction. It says, "Do the next right thing". The man holding the sign stops walking and just stands there looking at Matthew. Another man walks up behind him and stops and stares as well. His sign says, "Open your eyes." Another one says, "The signs are all around you."

This startles Matthew. He never has parades in front of his house. And the timing seems surreal and intentional. He slowly lifts his hand and waves at the two men. As he does police cars surround the parade and start to break it up. Police officers rush straight towards the two men and scoot them away. Just then his phone rings. It is an acquaintance from his past. He closes the blinds and answers his phone. "Yes sir. How can I help you?"

"Matthew. This is Evan Joshua. I don't know if you remember me. I did a few shows for you back in 2015. I didn't know much back then but you taught me a lot and you were kind to me. I heard you were thinking about getting out of corporate video. I don't know if you know this but I started flipping houses. It is hard work, but it is very fulfilling to see the transformation take place. So what do you say? Are you going to sit around and get fat? Or do you want to help both of us out?"

Matthew is still in a daze from the timing of this phone call. He lifts up one of the blinds to look outside and he sees a sign on the ground that says, "What are you waiting for?" It takes his breath away and then he replies, "Evan. I remember you. Congratulations on your new business. How can I help?"

Evan is reluctant, "I know this is probably beneath you, but I wanted to offer it to you first. I am tired of having a lot of stupid people that don't understand the value of quality work so I fired them all. I just want one person who gets it. I can train you to do the work. That's easy. I just can't train someone to actually care and I know that you do. What do you say?"

Matthew knows this would mean much harder work and much less money than he is used to. But he looks down at the sign again and agrees to give it a shot. He couldn't think of how taking this menial job would help make the world a better place, but he was trying to step out in faith and walk a path that he couldn't see. How could he go from influencing millions of people every day to helping one guy with one house at a time? Would that really make any difference at all? It didn't seem to make sense, but all the signs he asked for were there so he proceeded.

The next morning Matthew showed up to a dirty, cluttered house to meet Evan. As they walked through the house Matthew was rethinking his decision to help Evan. There were huge piles of trash everywhere. There were holes in the walls. It smelled like an outhouse on a hot summer day. Several doors had been kicked in. Light fixtures were missing. The floors hadn't been updated since the late 70's.

Rats and roaches scurried off when they walked into a room. There was graffiti on the walls. There was literally a barrel in one of the bedrooms that a hobo had used to burn trash to keep warm. All the walls and ceiling were black in that room. Matthew was used to a clean, organized environment. He was used to five star hotels and fancy catering and limousines. This was all a bit jarring to him. He was trying to smile, but he looked disgusted.

Evan was used to the filth. He patted Matthew on the back firmly and said, "What do you think buddy? It has a lot of potential doesn't it? It has good bones. I'm sure you can see the vision I have here."

Matthew didn't want to touch anything. He said, "Yeah, I'm more of an idea person. I can tell you what you need to do to make it beautiful again."

Evan laughed loudly, "I don't need an idea person brother. I know what I need to do. I need someone to help me shovel this garbage out of here and wade through the filth with me until this hobo shack is transformed into the nicest place in the neighborhood. There are some gloves over there. Help me pick this piece up. I have a dumpster out back."

It was at this moment that Matthew realized the gravity of the situation. He wasn't hired for his head. He was hired for his back. In his mind he determined to finish the day out with Evan since he had already committed to it and then conveniently have some other crisis arise that wouldn't allow him to come back... ever!

Evan was easy going and friendly. He was very happy to have Matthew helping him work. They laughed and joked around a lot. They reminisced about shows they had worked and how crazy the industry could be. The work was hard. There was no doubt about that. But the time passed quickly. Before Matthew knew it they were eating lunch.

Corporate shows were nothing like that. It was a lot of high stress and unnecessary pressure for nothing. You could never get a straight answer. You were a cog in a wheel on a need to know basis. And time dragged on. Five hours would seem to pass and you would look at the clock and it had only been three minutes.

As the day went on Matthew became aware that he was actually enjoying himself. By quitting time they had cleaned out all the trash from the house, patched holes in the walls, and scraped the floors. They had also caulked and prepped for paint the next day. His body was tired, but he felt alive for the first time in a long time.

There was something strangely satisfying about making something beautiful out of something that had been disgusting. It wasn't beautiful yet, but he could actually see the potential and it kind of excited him. No one was there to criticize or to praise their work. The world was not a better place because of what they had done. But his world was.

Evan handed Matthew a few hundred dollars and smiled. "Thank you for helping me today. I know it isn't the kind of money you are used to. Do you feel up to doing it again tomorrow?"

Matthew looked at the cash in his hand. He looked around at the progress they had made in just one day and said, "You know what. Why not? I'll be here in the morning."

Matthew slept well that night. He didn't overthink his life. He wasn't stressed. He wasn't searching for answers. Honestly he was just plain tired and his body needed the rest.

The next morning he showed up early to the jobsite. He was in the habit of being early. He was used to sayings like, "15 minutes early is late" and "A minute late and you're out the gate". As he walked up to the house he noticed the door was slightly ajar. He didn't think anything of it. He just walked inside and started looking for Evan.

He noticed fresh graffiti on the walls and it smelled like spray paint. As he turned the corner he was startled to see human feces in the middle of the hallway. He heard someone in the other room trying to open a window. His adrenaline kicked in as he realized that there was an intruder in the house.

He grabbed a hammer and held it claw side out. Whoever this criminal was he had broken in to their house and messed up what they just worked so hard to fix. Matthew was prepared to hurt this guy, whoever he was.

He peaked around the doorway and saw a young mother with a dirty toddler trying to get the window open. They smelled like they hadn't showered in weeks. They had windburn and chapped lips. They both looked exhausted and hopeless. The toddler saw Matthew and started screaming and crying.

The mother looked terrified. She tried to comfort her child but was also cowering while she looked at Matthew. "Please don't call the police. We was just cold is all. I'm real sorry."

Matthew was angry, "Why? Why did you break in this house? Why did you have to spray paint the walls? We just worked so hard to fix them. Why did you poop in the hall? I mean seriously, who does that?"

"There weren't no toilet and my baby takes his diaper off sometimes and just goes wherever he pleases. Rich kids do it too. Don't judge me."

Matthew was shocked, "and the spray paint?" She hung her head, "I don't know. I'm just mad I guess. Life ain't easy. I'm sorry."

Matthew evaluated the situation. A part of him wanted to hurt them for messing up what he worked so hard to fix. After all they were criminals. Well, she was at least. He should call the cops. That would be the right thing to do. Maybe she could get a shower and a meal and straighten her life out if she went to jail?

Maybe a nice family with a stable home could adopt that kid? He remembered the sign that said, "Do the next right thing." He wondered what the right thing to do is in this situation. He closed his eyes for a quick second and quietly asked for guidance. Before he could open his eyes he felt a hand on his shoulder. It was Evan.

Evan seemed a lot more used to this sort of thing. "What's your name, Hon?"

"I ain't gotta tell you nothin'" she fired back.

Evan was empathetic, "You are right. You don't have to tell me your name. I get it. Well look, my name is Evan and this is Matthew. You look hungry. What if we took you up to the truck stop? You could get a meal and a shower and a little rest. How does that sound?"

Matthew stood in awe. This woman had ruined his work and literally crapped on his floor and he didn't seem the least bit upset. And then he offered to feed her and help her out? Matthew didn't know how to react.

The woman was ashamed, "My baby is pretty hungry and I guess I am too. I could really use a shower. Why are you helping me? I ain't never did nothin' for you."

Evan smiled, "Because if I were you I would want me to help. You look like you have had a hard run. Let us help you. Come on."

"Well let me get my stuff together real quick." She looked at the floor, "Let me clean up this mess first. I'm real sorry. My baby is acting out. I think he is confused. My baby daddy beat me and so I left him, but I've been too ashamed to go back to my parents house so we've been living on the streets for a few months now." She started crying while she cleaned up the floor.

Matthew put the hammer down. "Here, I'll get that." Matthew cleaned up the mess on the floor while she gathered her things. "Sharon. My name is Sharon. And my baby is Bobby."

Matthew's heart was broken for this poor woman. He was ready to hurt her or put her in jail because he was angry and afraid, but now he just wanted to help her.

They all shared a meal together. The more they talked the more Matthew realized she wasn't some demon. She was a girl who had been hurt and was trying to survive in a very difficult situation. After she had showered and eaten Evan handed her $50 and asked her not to break into any more houses. As she was about to leave Matthew spoke up, "Can we just call your parents and tell them you are ok? I'm sure they are worried about you." The girl paused and turned around with tears in her eyes, " I would like that very much."

Matthew let her use his phone and she called her parents. They were so happy to hear from her. They agreed to come and pick her up immediately. While they waited Matthew and Evan encouraged the young mother. In what seemed like no time the parents arrived. They thanked Matthew and Evan for their kindness and took their daughter and their grandson home.

After the family had driven off Evan sniffled and said, "Well, that wasn't how I expected to start the day. We lost a little time to do that, but it was worth it. What are the odds that she ended up in our house this morning? That could have gone a lot differently. We could have spent all morning dealing with the cops and her life and our day would have been ruined, but instead this became a story of redemption and hope. We will make up the time somehow. Things will work out. Of course, I'll still start your time at seven. I'll pay you for your time. It wasn't your fault this happened."

Matthew didn't know what to say. He was shocked. "Why are you so generous? You sacrificed your time, you bought us all breakfast, you paid the person who broke in and vandalized your house, you helped her reunite with her family, and then you want to pay me to sit there and watch all this kindness unfold? Absolutely not! I feel like I owe you.

I was ready to hurt or kill that girl. At the very least I was going to call the cops and put her in jail. I feel like we helped save that girl's life. And that baby has a chance at a real life now. I haven't done anything that meaningful in, well, I don't know if I ever have done anything like that. Wow! That feels really good. Why do I feel so good right now?"

Evan smiled, "Because when you help your brother across the river you end up across the river too. When you help someone else it is impossible to not end up helping yourself. Love is contagious brother. Come on. Let's get back to the job. We have a lot to do today."

The rest of the workday was very productive. They easily cleaned up the mess from the morning. Taped off the house and sprayed two coats of paint on the entire inside of the house. Matthew was shocked at how fast it all happened. Evan acted like this was perfectly normal. While the first coat was drying they went and bought fans and light fixtures. After they sprayed the second coat they hung all the fans and lights. They discussed what still needed to be done on the house.

Evan explained how they probably only had another two weeks left on this house, but he would have other projects coming up once this one sold. Matthew asked a lot of questions and Evan was happy to answer them all. In short Evan was able to do all this because he paid cash for the house. Because the house was uninsurable when he bought it he just assumed the risk, but he felt pretty confident that nothing too bad would happen. With the cost of the house and materials and paying his help he needed the house to sell quickly to keep going. He was stretched pretty thin financially, but he knew it would work out and be worth it in the end.

As they talked Evan installed new shower faucets. He soldered them and checked for leaks. Evan seemed to know what he was doing. Just before the day ended he soldered some shut off valves in the kitchen. They were close to the wall. The wall caught on fire but Evan kept working calmly and then blew out the flame. He tested for leaks and then called it a day. They locked up the house and walked out.

Matthew had developed a huge amount of respect for Evan in their short time together. Evan inspired him. Evan knew so much about so much. And he had such kindness and wisdom. He had no hidden agenda. He just genuinely enjoyed helping people and fixing things. Once again Matthew agreed to come work the next day.

He slept well that night. His anxiety had vanished. He wasn't stressed out or high strung. He felt at peace. It was a nice change. He looked forward to the next day and seeing what all they would do. He really enjoyed watching the house transform. He wondered who would live there. He wondered if they would appreciate the love that went into rebuilding their home. He wondered if they would know what a great man had worked so hard for total strangers to have a nice home. And then he fell asleep.

3 Which Path?

Matthew woke up early as he was in the habit of doing. He bought donuts and coffee for himself and Evan. There was a lot of traffic near the flip house. He was concerned about being late. Not that Evan would even care, but Matthew did. He wanted to live his life with honor. He had to park a few blocks away because the road was closed. As he walked closer he saw flashing lights. There were first responders all over the place. He hoped whoever was in trouble would be ok. He even said a prayer for them, whoever they were. He felt a little self-righteous as he did.

When he turned the corner he stopped. He dropped the donuts and coffee as his arms dropped to his side. He just stared unbelievingly. His eyes swelled with tears. He dropped his head. The house that they had been working on had burned to the ground over night. Everything was gone. Everything. He looked over and saw Evan talking to the fire department. He was distraught, but calm. Matthew's heart broke for Evan. He knew that the house was uninsured. He knew that Evan didn't have any more money to give. This would ruin him. Why did such a bad thing happen to such a good man? This just didn't seem fair. Matthew was angry. Who had done this? Why?

Evan looked over at Matthew and tried to smile. He held up his finger as if to say "Let me finish with the authorities. I'll be right there." He finished talking with them and walked slowly over to Matthew. "Man, I'm so sorry. I don't think we will have any work today. It might be awhile." He pulled out his wallet and started counting money. "I can pay you for today since you are already here. I should have called you. I apologize."

Matthew was in shock again. "Are you kidding me? I can't take your money. Put that away. I'm insulted. What kind of a man do you think I am?"

Evan had tears in his eyes, "I don't know what I'm going to do. I don't...I don't have any more money. I was floating a lot of these expenses on credit cards. I can't afford to rebuild every thing. I think I'm ruined."

Matthew asked, "What happened? Was it arson?"

"No. It was my fault. When I was soldering last night the wall caught fire and I blew it out. It happens all the time. I should have gone back and double checked, but I was tired and I knew you were too. It must have been smoldering in the wall and eventually caught fire. And now, this." Evan waves his hand at the destruction. "There is no one to blame but myself. I did this. I'm lucky I'm not going to jail."

Matthew didn't know what to say. He wanted to help, but had no words. He remembered the conference from a few nights before. He was reaching for answers but he just kept coming up blank. So he stood there awkwardly in silence.

After a long pause Evan lifted his head and said, "I know everything happens for a reason. I don't know what that reason is, but in the end it will make sense and will be part of the beautiful tapestry that God is weaving together from all of our lives. I just wish I hadn't been so stupid." He looked down at the ground and shook his head. "You don't have to stay Matthew. This isn't your problem. I appreciate all that you have done to help me these last few days. Now you can go and do something that matters more than my stupid flip house."

Matthew was in a daze, "Evan, I don't know if I have ever seen someone as generous and honorable as you. Yesterday someone broke in your house and you helped her to get her life back on track. You weren't upset at all. Then you tried to pay me to watch your kindness. I mean, who does that? And then we worked hard the rest of the day. I know I'm not that good at this stuff, but you were still generous and kind to me.

I know I wasn't worth what you paid me. We both know you have been over paying me. I'm grateful but I'm not stupid. And now after everything you have is gone and you are faced with despair you smile through the pain and are concerned for me? Man, why aren't you mad? I am angry for you. It's not fair."

Evan responded, "Life isn't fair Matthew. Life is filled with trials and temptations. It is filled with injustice and undeserved pain. I can choose to focus on all the bad things in life. I can choose to lose hope. I can lose my temper. I can yell and lash out. I can blame everyone else in the world beside myself for my problems.

I can stew in anger and waste away inside. I can rot in my soul, but I choose not to. Because there are also many good things in life and I choose to focus on them. Growth never happens on the mountaintops. It is always in the valleys. In the hard times we grow. We level up. We gain strength.

We are being watched you know. Someone sees me as their hero and I need to deserve that. A hero isn't defined by how he does in easy times. He is defined by how he responds in times like these. And so yes, it is hard. But I believe a way will be made and something beautiful will become of all this tragedy."

Matthew was having a real inner struggle with these words. This was how people should be, but he had never actually seen someone do it in real life. He didn't know how it would end. He remembered the list of good deeds from the conference and one kept echoing in his head "Give away something that is precious to you."

He would never say it out loud, but his money was very precious to him. He had worked very hard for it. He had sacrificed his life to work in a mundane industry to attain the security that his money afforded him now. He certainly didn't want to lose it. He had a few hundred thousand dollars saved from all of his years of hard work. He had lived with less to be able to save that money. He thought for a moment that he could help Evan to overcome this obstacle, but quickly dismissed the thought as offensive. Surely some other way would be made. This wasn't even his responsibility.

Matthew tried to comfort Evan, "Maybe we could do a GoFundMe?"

Evan shook his head, "I appreciate the offer. I won't do that. I won't ask for strangers to pay for my mistake. I'll just have to go work for someone and hope I can crawl out of this hole without going bankrupt. I will pay back my debt no matter what. It is the right thing to do. This is going to take a long time to recover from. It's going to sting for a while."

Matthew was perplexed, "Do you have anything you could sell to get the money? Maybe cash in your 401k? Mortgage another house? Inheritance money?"

"I already did all that. That's how I was able to buy this house in the first place. I'm tapped out brother. I have nothing, nothing but debt. And a burned down house." Evan replied. "Don't worry about it. It isn't your problem. I'm sure you will find some other work. You are very skilled."

Matthew was really struggling, "OK look. How much are we talking about here, to get the house sellable I mean?"

Evan puts some numbers together in his head, "This is a big set back. It will probably cost $150,000."

Matthew cringed, "What if I could loan you the money until the house sells?"

Evan was shocked, "I would never ask you to do that."

Matthew relaxed a little, "Yeah, I know you wouldn't. And I know you will do everything in your power to pay me back as soon as possible. I want to help. I feel like this is a crossroads in your life. I feel like you can do so much, but this could crush you. Let me help you a little to get over this hump. You can pay me back when the house sells."

It took Evan's breath away, "You would do that for me? But why?"

Matthew started to warm up to the idea, "I believe in you Evan. Maybe one day I will need someone to be kind to me. Today I can be kind to you and I want to." He stuck his hand out to shake Evan's hand. "Will you let me help you Evan? Please?"

Evan had tears streaming down his face, "Only if we can split the profit once the house sells. I won't let you take a risk without the potential for reward. I can't tell you how much this means to me. I'll write up a contract that outlines how I will repay you. You can have a lien on the property until I pay you back to protect your investment."

"That won't be necessary. If I didn't trust you I wouldn't have offered to help you. I know you are a man of your word. I have already seen that. A handshake is fine with me." Matthew smiled and reached out his hand to Evan. Evan shook his hand.

It felt as if a huge weight had been lifted off of Matthew. He didn't know how to explain it. He should have been worried or at the very least apprehensive. But instead he felt... joy and an indescribable peace. Seeing the relief in Evan's eyes was such a huge reward. He seemed to know that he made a difference in this man's life. Far more than all of his "important" work ever did.

It was strange to him, but the more he said yes to these difficult situations the happier he became. He wanted to do even more. The feeling of helping others was becoming habit forming. He looked over at the smoldering building and then looked up to the sky and smiled as if to say "Thank you for allowing me this opportunity. Thank you for letting me be a blessing to someone who deeply deserved it and had no other hope."

Once the fire department left Evan and Matthew immediately started a plan of action to rebuild. They both seemed excited. "There are a few things that could be better and now we have the chance to make it all right. This house is going to be awesome!" Evan is excited to see the transformation "We should take some pictures of it now while it looks horrible so that we can tell the story of redemption once it is beautiful!"

And so they do. They take pictures of all the rubble and of themselves standing in front of it smiling. They are smiling because they have hope and they have something to believe in. They have a common goal. They can see past the tragedy to the end when everything will be far better than it was before. And so the project went on for the next two months. It all went together very quickly. Matthew helped with everything. He was no longer a paid helper. Now he was a partner with a vested interest in the success of this home.

He learned so much as they worked together. He learned about how houses were made. He learned what made them withstand the hardships of weather and time. He learned about integrity and generosity and kindness and honor. He also learned about himself and how much more he was capable of. He became stronger physically, mentally, and spiritually. Was it hard? Sure. But it was worth it! Matthew loved every minute of it.

The time passed much too quickly and before they knew it the project was finished. The house sold almost immediately. It didn't even go on the market. Someone came by as they were doing the finishing touches and said they had been watching the whole thing. They loved the house and wanted to make an offer that was higher than market value before anyone else snatched it up.

Matthew got back all the money he invested, he was paid back for his time, and he made a nice profit. In the long run he ended up making more money doing this grunt work than he would have doing "important" video work for corporations. Needless to say Evan was very grateful. He had avoided bankruptcy and was able to do quite well on the house even with the huge financial set back of the fire.

Once the house sold and the checks were deposited Evan took Matthew out to eat, "You saved me Matthew. I can't let it go unsaid. I don't know if I ever would have recovered from the fire financially, but because of you here we are. You are a real friend. If you ever need anything from me, anything at all, don't hesitate to ask. I am forever in your debt."

Matthew smiles, "Evan, let's be honest. You have all the skills and the tools. I was just an overpaid helper. I should be the one thanking you. I thought I would be taking a hit by working with you, but in the end I made better money than I have ever made in my life. I learned a lot. I lost my gut and got some muscles. And I learned so much about the important things in life. You are a real treasure. I have learned the joy of selflessness because of you. I was so lost for so long and now I feel like I am on the road home. Thank you."

Evan responds with a smile, "Matthew Jacobs, you have just leveled up. From now on your kindness will lead to your success. Never forget that. Don't choose the easy road. Choose the right one. Listen carefully. Let your conscience be your guide. Love the unlovely. Remember that. Love the unlovely. It is important that you know that. Look for the person that nobody wants to love and seek to help them."

Matthew smiles "That is one thing I have learned from you Evan. How to love the... Hmm? That was one of the things on the list at that last conference I did. Love the unlovely. It was one of the good deeds. If he stepped on that piece of paper he avoided being alone forever and the reward was... What was it?"

Evan interrupts without thinking, "Find the love of your life."

This shocks Matthew. "Did I tell you the list? Wow! Weird? Wait? How did you know that? I think that is what it was. Have I told you about that conference?"

Evan gets nervous and starts to answer, "I can't lie to you, but..." Evan's phone rings and he answers "Hello. Yes, I know but. Yeah, I slipped. I don't know what I was thinking. OK. I understand." He ends the call. "Matthew that is all I can say about this right now. I have to go. I won't see you again in this life. Stay strong brother. We all believe in you." He looks down at a text message. "I have to go. It has been a pleasure spending this time with you. Remember to love the unlovely."

Evan pays the bill and walks out. Matthew is very confused. He wants to get up and follow Evan. He wants to ask him what in the world he is talking about, but he feels glued to his chair. As if he couldn't get up even if he wanted to. Matthew has a lot of questions about what Evan has just said. He can't for the life of him remember ever talking to Evan about the conference or the lists.

How could he have known the next thing on the list? How could he have just rattled it off so quickly like that without a thought? Why did his phone ring at exactly that point in the conversation? What did that text message say? And why wouldn't he see him again in this life? None of this made any sense at all to Matthew. He assumed they would do another flip house and continue their adventure together. This seemed to be his calling. He was good at it. Suddenly though Matthew felt like he was being watched.

He looked around the restaurant and all the people seemed to be staring at him. The music stopped. A man across the room looks at Matthew and then looks down at his table. Matthew looks down at the table and Evan had left a note that said, "Leave now!" He felt compelled to leave and all of the sudden he could move again so he quickly left the restaurant. He walks down the street but felt as if everyone was watching him still so he ducked into an alley and hid behind a dumpster. He became very tired and he quickly fell asleep.

4 Better Than I Thought

Matthew is awakened from his sleep by the sounds of a struggle. He opens his eyes to see three young men punching and kicking a hobo. The hobo is crying. His mouth is bleeding. He has a black eye. The thugs are relentless. For a moment Matthew fears for his own life. He looks and there is an easy way for him to escape unharmed and unnoticed. This isn't his fight. Perhaps this guy has done something to deserve this beating. One of the thugs has a gun. It isn't his problem. He considers running away for a moment, but then he stops himself. How could he even think about not helping this man? He is better than that. The old Matthew probably would have just turned and walked away. Matthew gathers his courage, takes a deep breath and stands up.

Matthew shouts loudly and with authority, "Hey! Stop hurting him!"

The thugs stop for a moment. They turn and look at Matthew. One of them raises his gun toward Matthew. "This isn't your fight. Walk away."

Another one chimes in "Yeah, don't try to be a hero. You might end up a dead hero. What good would that do?"

The third one grabs a bottle and smashes it against a brick wall. Holding the broken part he points it towards Matthew and steps forward. "You don't want any of this. Turn around and leave. Forget you saw any of this."

Matthew looks scared. He has never had his life threatened like this before. He considers walking away. He thinks about all he has to live for. Really the choice is simple. It is between some random stranger's life that nobody cares about and his own precious life. This guy may not even deserve his sacrifice. These guys may kill the hobo after they kill Matthew anyway. He sees the gravity of the situation. He weighs the possibilities. He thinks of every excuse he can to leave, and then he decides to stay anyway.

"What has this man done to you? Matthew asks.

"He stinks! He is ugly. He is a cancer on our society. He is worthless. Who even cares about this guy?" one of the thugs yells.

The hobo cowers beneath them. He is crying as he wipes blood from his eyes. He spits out a piece of broken tooth. "They are right" he says, "Just let me die. I don't want to live any more anyway."

"See. He wants to die. Walk away and save yourself." The thug with the broken bottle shouts as he moves closer to the hobo. He pulls his arm back as he is about to strike.

Matthew is stunned, "Nobody wants to die? They only want the pain to end. They just don't want to keep on living like this. I can't stand by and do nothing. Leave him alone."

"Or what?" laughs the guy with the gun.

"Or you will have to kill me first." Matthew says sadly.

"Have it your way." One of them yells out. Another one sucker punches Matthew in the face hard. Matthew falls to the ground. They laugh and turn back around to the hobo. "Now where were we?"

Matthew took a heavy hit that shakes him hard. He looks through the blood running down his forehead and sees them about to attack the hobo again. He drops his head as he braces himself for more pain and then rises up to his feet. "Stop!" he yells.

"Or what? What are you going to do about it?" the thug with the gun shouts in his face.

"I'm not dead yet." Matthew says to him bravely.

The thug pistol whips Matthew and knocks him to the ground. "We can change that real quick." He points the gun at Matthew. "Is this unlovable piece of trash worth your life?"

Matthew has tears in his eyes. He prepares himself to die. "Yes. He is. Do what you have to do." Matthew closes his eyes and hears the gun cock back. He gulps but remains steadfast. "Stay strong Matthew. Don't be a coward." He whispers to himself.

"Give me your wallet first and your cell phone." The guy with the gun says.

One of the thugs pushes the gun away from Matthew's head slowly. "We can't do this. We have gone too far already. You have to let him have this one. You know the rules."

Just then a whistle blows from the street. "Cops!" one of them yells. They run away down the alley and police officers run right past Matthew and the hobo after the thugs.

Matthew opens his eyes and it is just him and the hobo in the alley. The hobo is stunned, "You almost just died bro." Matthew nods slowly "You almost just died... for me? I don't even know you man. Who does that? I can't give you anything. You know that right? I wish I could, but I'm poor. I don't have anything."

"You don't owe me anything. How could I stand by and do nothing? What kind of a man does that?" Matthew replies as he wipes blood from his face.

"Most people wouldn't have even looked up from their phones to see me, but you. You were about to take a bullet for me..." the hobo has tears in his eyes "Why would you do that? Don't you have anyone that loves you?"

Matthew thinks for a moment. What an odd question. "Of course people love me."

"I don't see a ring on your finger." The hobo scoffs "Do you have a girlfriend?"

"No. But even if I did I would have done the same thing." Matthew replies. "What is your name anyway?"

"My name is Stephen." He stands up quickly and offers his hand to Matthew. "Nice to make your acquaintance."

"I'm Matthew. It's a pleasure to meet you Stephen. Do you have family that could help you? Those bruises look pretty bad."

"My mom is dead. I never knew my dad. I lived with my uncle for a while when I was a teenager, but he molested me so I ran away. I have a half sister, but I haven't seen her in years."

"I can call her if you want. I'm sure she is worried about you." Matthew pulls out his phone.

Stephen laughs under his breath, "Doubtful. Nobody cares about me. I'm worthless."

Matthew hugs Stephen "No sir. You are not worthless. Don't think that even for a second. God doesn't make junk. I'm sure there is some reason why I ended up here with you today. Let's call her. Do you know her number?"

"I have it written down somewhere." He pulls out a crumpled piece of paper from his duffle bag. Matthew dials the number for Stephen and hands him the phone.

"Is this Lacey?" Stephen says hesitantly

"Stephen? Is that you? I have been so worried about you. Where are you? Are you in trouble?" Lacey asks eagerly.

"No. I'm fine. Well I'm a little banged up right now. These three guys were beating me up and someone came along and" he whimpers, "and saved my life." He starts to cry. "He just stood in front of a gun for me Lacey. He doesn't even know me."

"Stephen, I'm so happy you are alive. Tell me where you are and I'll come get you right now."

"I don't want to be a burden. You don't have to do that. I'm sure you are busy. I can heal alone. There is a shelter that will help me for a while if I'm hurt real bad. Shelters don't like helping men much, but if I'm hurt bad enough I can stay until I am mostly better. I've done it before."

"Are you? Are you hurt badly? Send me an address. I'm on my way." She says with a sense of urgency.

Before long a beautiful girl comes running around the corner and hugs Stephen's neck. She looks at him and says, "What took you so long to call me? How long have you been here? Let's get you cleaned up. You need a shower." She puts her arm around him and starts walking him around the corner to her car.

Matthew stands up and dusts off his pants. He winces as he touches the newly forming scab on his forehead. Despite the pain he feels good inside his soul. Someone really loved Stephen and he got to help reunite them. Who even knew what a difference that could make in the world? He was just happy to have gotten to be a part of that. His face would heal, but the ripples from this experience would live on and he was grateful for that. This was part of the adventure that his life was becoming.

As he is walking out from the alley he remembers what Evan had said about loving the unlovely and he smiles at the sky. "I did it Evan." He whispers to himself. Just then Lacey comes running back around the corner.

"Well, are you coming or what?" she says to Matthew "I thought you were following me. Please. You just saved my brother's life. Let me make you dinner as a thank you. I know it isn't much, but let me show my gratitude to you."

"How can I say no to an offer like that?" Matthew shyly replies. "I mean if I won't be intruding."

So Matthew had dinner with Lacey and Stephen. Stephen didn't say much. He kept to himself. It turns out that Stephen had a breakdown and had been homeless for quite some time. Lacey was his only living relative. She was very grateful to have her brother back. The more Matthew and Lacey talked the more he wanted to know about her. They seemed to have a real connection.

She seemed very familiar to him, like maybe they had known each other in another life. She was easy to talk to and she was easy on the eyes. Lacey was a very pretty girl. She was kind. She was sweet and helpful. She was single. And she seemed to like Matthew as well. Her body language leaned in to him. She laughed at his jokes and touched his arm every chance she got.

Something you should probably know about Matthew is that he has been hurt in love a lot. At this point in his life he has no real hope of ever having a special girl in his life again. It hardly even seems worth it to him. He has been cheated on and left more times then he cares to mention. Every time he becomes vulnerable with a girl she uses all of his weaknesses against him. And it never ends well. So he has wrapped his heart in razor wire and let it get cold and hard. He has hidden it far away where it can never be found again. Locked behind layers of steel doors and a gauntlet of obstacles that will protect it from intruders. But sadly his heart cries alone most days hidden behind busyness and a smile.

This isn't something he shares with anyone. He knows that if he talks about it that someone will make a project out of him and try to "help". He doesn't want that. His heart wants to be left alone to slowly die in peace. But beneath the facade he anxiously hopes that someone will see his true value and show him the love that he so desperately needs. In reality he has a soft kind heart that is covered in layers of scars and callouses that have become seemingly impenetrable. And although Lacey is a beautiful girl who Matthew could see possibly spending the rest of his life with he simply thanks her for dinner and goes on his way. He feels that he is probably letting the love of his life slip away, but he is afraid. So he leaves and assumes he will never see her again.

That night he stares at his phone hoping she will call or text, but she doesn't. She can't. Neither does he. He struggles wondering what the next right thing to do is. He wants to see her again. He wants to melt through the pain that covers his heart, but he almost wants someone else to force his hand. Because when it fails he can blame someone else beside himself. He just can't bring himself to initiate a conversation with her. He starts to text her several times but then deletes everything and just stares at his phone overthinking the entire situation. Sadly, she was at home alone doing the same thing. So days past and life became busy again and they continued to long for each other while neither one of them would do anything about it.

Matthew's face eventually healed, but he was left with a scar under his eye where he had been pistol-whipped. Lacey took care of her brother and gave him a place to heal. Every time she looked at him she was reminded of Matthew and every time Matthew saw the scar on his face he thought of her. Two souls who longed for each other but refused to be hurt again also missed out on love while experiencing deeply the very pain they were trying to avoid. And sadness remained a part of their existence.

In the meantime Matthew was trying to continue his journey to find meaning in his life. He had started volunteering at a homeless shelter. He really developed a heart for the hurting. An opportunity arose for him to go and help and so he assumed this was the next right thing and he said yes. People told him he was brave for going, but he just wondered how he could even consider not going. It didn't make sense to him. If someone needed his help and he was able, he figured it was his obligation to do so. It had been six months since Matthew left his career and his mindset had changed completely. He wasn't seeking a bigger paycheck any more. He believed with all his heart that he could be the answer to someone's prayers.

He knew that there were people he prayed for and he longed for someone to show kindness to them. So he lived his life in such a way that he could be the answer to other people's prayers. He wanted to be the hands and feet of God. He had learned to look for opportunities to help people every chance he got. It gave him great joy. And somehow a way was always provided for him. When he stepped out in faith the doors just opened up and he walked through them. There was no need to worry.

5 Choices, Choices

He had learned to navigate the signs to some degree. He noticed that when there was something important and life changing coming that it would be met with great opposition. His life would seem to be cluttered with distractions and roadblocks. It was as if the entire universe was screaming at him to not do what he was about to do. But if he would just quiet himself and pay attention there was a clear path through all the chaos that was actually much simpler than all the alternatives being offered.

It took tremendous strength of character to push through the resistance but over time he learned that the rewards were worth the effort. Just to be clear these were not monetary rewards at all. There was a real pleasure in helping a person even in the simplest of ways. It became habit forming for him. Of course when the breakthroughs were bigger that was great too. Just being able to smile at a stranger and brighten their day seemed to also brighten his day. Matthew was discovering how to truly live. And what he was doing was contagious. It took a while at first but he started to notice people around him acting differently too.

When he first arrived at the homeless shelter it seemed dark and sad and gloomy. But he got in the habit of looking for things to be thankful for, things to be happy about. Funny thing about seeking goodness is that you will find it if you look. It is everywhere. It also seemed like the more he helped people with their lives the more he unlocked secrets to living his own life more fully.

One particular day an old war veteran had lost control of his bowels. Nobody wanted to clean up the mess. Matthew didn't either. When nobody volunteered he saw the sadness in the old man's face and he said, "I'll do it." He was discreet and treated the man with dignity. Very few words were exchanged, but he knew he had made a difficult and embarrassing situation much easier for someone who could no longer help himself. He hoped that one day, if he ever needed it, someone would help him.

Later that night Matthew walked into his room and a thought occurred to him. When he went to turn on a light he never wondered if the darkness would overpower the light. There wasn't really a struggle between darkness and light or good and evil. This was life changing to him.

Darkness is not the opposite of light. Darkness is the absence of light. Cold is not the opposite of heat. Cold is the absence of heat. You can't add cold to something. You can only remove heat and cold is what is left.

And evil is not the opposite of good. Evil is the absence of good. Once a light is on the darkness disappears instantly. Once good enters a room evil flees as well. The only time that darkness prevails is when there is no light. The absence of light creates a void and all that is left is darkness. The same must be true of good and evil.

And so, if we live in a dark and evil world then that is on us for not letting our light shine. More specifically it was on him. Matthew took this knowledge as a responsibility to let his light shine in such a way so that no darkness could exist around him. He would no longer hide his light under a bushel.

He would quietly observe patterns in other people's lives that led both to their glory and to their destruction. Once he felt he had an answer he would first apply it to his own life to test it and see if it was true. After he had found solutions to the problems that were plaguing him he would share generously with anyone who would listen.

Not in a preachy judgmental way but gently as a friend would help a friend. In fact, Matthew became a great friend to everyone he met. He was an inspiration. It had become so rare for someone to actually live out their faith that it took most people by surprise. Some were turned off by it. After a lifetime of conditioning to only respond with insults and sarcasm a lot of people simply didn't know how to take him.

That didn't stop him at all. He loved helping people. He loved hearing their stories. He loved seeing hope in their eyes. He loved watching lives transform over time for the better. Day after day he wanted more and more to do all he could to make the world, his world, a better place.

One of the biggest rewards he enjoyed was when someone else decided to let their light shine as well. When unprompted they took matters into their own hands and chose to bless people. To see the light bulb go on inside someone became his greatest joy. It seemed as though he would become unstoppable and he was well on his way when it happened. He met Jade.

Jade was everything every guy would ever want. She was smoking hot, sexy, fun loving, and easy to get along with. And she was famous. She was on every billboard in town. She was the face and the voice of the media.

By this time the hope of Lacey had faded, although he still thought about her several times a day. He just never actually reached out to her. If he had he would have realized that she wanted to see him too. But believing this one lie opened up a world of hurt for Matthew, one that grew inside of him. He tried to suppress it. He tried to stay busy and keep her out of his head. But when the stillness came and there were no more distractions it would haunt him.

Rather than just calling her he would think of all the bad things that could happen. He would talk himself out of it. He succumbed to lies that he wasn't good enough or that she wasn't worth the hassle. His deep loneliness amidst a huge crowd of people haunted him and so he didn't sleep much. Surrounded by friends, with everything to be thankful for, there was sadness behind his smile.

He had seen pictures of Jade everywhere he went for months. She was on magazine covers and advertisements. She was typically wearing very little clothing and advertising things Matthew wouldn't buy or use. He pretended not to notice her, but that would have been impossible. She was everywhere he looked. She was a super model.

People talked about her often in front of Matthew. There would be all the typical lustful guy talk. Matthew would politely not say anything or find a reason to leave the conversation. There was no doubt that she was a sex symbol. Everyone knew it. In fact, apart from her looks Matthew knew very little about her. He had been alone for a very long time and although he didn't realize it he was vulnerable in this area. There was a chink in his armor.

One particular morning Matthew woke up early as he was in the habit of doing. He went for an early morning run. On his run he was planning his day and thinking about what he could do. There were no deadlines he had to meet. There was nothing he had to do that day necessarily. He was a little bored and was feeling lazy.

As he was thinking this he looked up at a billboard with Jade's picture on it. It said "Nothing to do today? Bored. Treat yourself to a massage. You deserve it." Matthew thought about the timing of him seeing this sign and laughed to himself about the irony of it all. As he continued to run he noticed how sore he was and he thought a massage did sound nice. He also thought how nice it would be to have a girl he loved pamper him. He quickly dismissed this thought and kept running.

There was a red light and so he paused and ran in place while he waited. He looked down and there was a coupon for a free massage on the ground with Jade's picture on it. He looked around but nobody had dropped it. He picked it up and was going to throw it away but the nearest trashcan was two blocks away so he put it in his pocket and kept running.

As he neared the trashcan his phone rang. He answered his phone and ran right past the trashcan. It was a robot asking about his car's extended warranty. He was mildly irritated but just kept running.

Suddenly he felt thirsty. He looked around and there was no place to get any water in sight except a trendy coffee shop. He rolled his eyes and was going to keep going, but there was a sign out front that said, "Dehydrated? Come inside and Rehydrate". It was a stupid ad, but well timed and so he stopped and got in line. As expected the line was filled with people all talking about first world problems.

"OMG! The last time I had this barista I asked for 2 pumps of caramel, but he put in 4 half pumps instead. I can't even today!" said a young girl in line ahead of him.

"Oh girl I want to show you this thing I found on Etsy. Ugh! My phone is at 1% and the Wi-Fi in here is archaic! What is this? The 1900's?"

"My credit card is almost maxed out and I need a manicure. Can you cover me? I'll totally get my dad to buy us new eyelashes later." One girl whined.

Matthew just wanted some water. This was more than a little irritating and the line was at least 20 minutes long. "Nope." He said to himself as he turned around to walk out. And that is when he bumped into Jade. She was standing behind him in line and he almost knocked her over in his haste to leave. "I'm so sorry ma'am" Matthew apologized. As he was saying this he realized who she was. She must have seen it on his face.

"Please don't make a big deal about it" Jade whispers. She puts her hand on his shoulder and looks him in the eyes. She smiles confidently. "We can just keep this between us right?"

Matthew is stunned. He nods slowly. "Can I buy your coffee in exchange for your discretion?" Jade says quietly.

"I don't drink coffee," Matthew mumbles awkwardly.

"Well I suppose you go to bars and don't drink alcohol too don't you?" She laughs.

"As a matter of fact I do." Matthew sighs.

Jade laughs out loud "Who does that? You are weird. I like you. Let me buy you a water at least or whatever it is you drink."

A moment ago Matthew wanted to leave as quickly as he could, but now he was under her spell. "I am very thirsty," he says.

It looks like Jade is trying to hide her identity, but not really. She is wearing yoga pants that show off her slender figure. She is wearing a tight shirt that says "Eye Candy" in bright big gold letters with bling all over her. She is wearing high heels and she has an expensive purse.

But she has on a baseball cap and large sunglasses. Her baseball cap says "Jade" on it. The fact that no one else in the coffee shop recognizes her is bewildering to Matthew. It is so obvious. But she seems to be invisible to them. Until it was time to pay and the cashier says, "It's on the house. Can I take a picture with you for Instagram?" Jade pretends to be bothered but smiles for the picture and says, "Tag me!"

"Thank you for the water ma'am" Matthew says politely as he begins to walk out.

"Ma'am is my mother's name. Aren't you going to walk me home? I did buy your drink. What if I get mugged?" Jade calls after him.

Matthew stops. He doesn't want to go with her because he feels tempted by her but she had pleaded with his goodness. He had seen someone mugged in that same area not all that long ago. Stephen, Lacey's brother. He knew Jade was a high profile target so he agreed to walk with her.

As they walk down the road Matthew notices every guy's head turn to follow her as they walk by. He hears comments about her body as they walk along. Several guys take out their phones and take pictures of her. "Ignore them. It happens all the time. You just get used to it after a while." Jade says.

"Doesn't that get old? Don't you want people to care about what is inside?" Matthew asks.

"I don't really care. I'm getting paid. People can think whatever they want. It doesn't affect me. Girls wish they could be me and guys wish they could be with me. It's a pretty easy life." Jade giggled. "It's like one long party that never ends and I'm the star!" She twirls around as she says this.

A construction crew starts whistling at her and screaming inappropriate things. Matthew yells back "She is someone's daughter you know."

Jade smiles, "Aww you are defending my honor. How sweet. Now take me home brave knight." She laughs. She grabs Matthew's arm and holds him as they walk. She looks up in his eyes. He looks at her for a minute like he is under a spell. It is hard to not notice how beautiful she is.

"Kiss her you idiot," someone yells from behind him. She looks longingly at him. He gathers himself and keeps walking. She holds onto his arm and pulls him close as they walk. Matthew is having an inner struggle. Obviously Jade is very attractive. Matthew still has feelings for Lacey. But how stupid is that? He only really met her one time. He is sure that she has moved on and is probably happy with someone else. She probably wouldn't like him anyway. And he has the girl that everyone wants throwing herself at him. What kind of a fool wouldn't jump on this opportunity? But why was she interested in him anyway? He isn't anything special.

He continued on with this train of thought the whole walk home. He really was lonely. He really wanted to have someone to love. Maybe this was his reward for all the good he had been doing? His younger self wouldn't have given any of this a second thought. He would have kissed that girl and taken her straight to bed. Most guys probably would.

Why was he so conflicted about this? What was the matter with him? He had a beautiful girl on his arm and all he could think about was another girl. Matthew was beyond distracted. He didn't want to make the wrong choice. Not that he had been given very many choices recently. Let's be honest the older a person gets the smaller the dating pool becomes. If a girl is the least bit interested you better at least give her a chance. It becomes more and more rare as time passes.

Once you get to a certain age dating is like going to the dump and trying to pick the least disgusting piece of trash to bring home with you that doesn't smell that bad. This girl wasn't trash. She was hot. Why was he having such a struggle? Even if they did start a relationship how hard would it be to have every other guy in the world wanting to be with your girl? How could it last? She traveled all the time for her work.

Matthew used to travel all the time too, but he had become a rather simple man. Did they even stand a chance of having a real relationship? What would have to change in his life if he were to start going out with her? Was it worth it? What a horrible thing to think! Was a person worth your time? Was a beautiful girl worth his time? Of course she was. All people are worth it. Aren't they?

In the meantime Jade talked nonstop. She seemed careless and at peace. She was right in her element. And she seemed to be very into Matthew for whatever reason. She made sure to keep hold of his arm the entire walk home. She kept touching him at every opportunity. She was very flattering with her words and flirtatious with her behavior. Matthew was smitten by her, but knew nothing about her at the same time. They finally arrived at her home. Matthew stopped and said "Thank you for the wonderful conversation. It was nice getting to know you."

"Aren't you going to come in?" Jade giggles. "We are having such a great time. Why does it have to end? I like talking to you. Come on." She tugs at his pants and the massage coupon falls out of his pocket. Jade looks down at the coupon and smiles. "I know her. She is hot. I'd do her." She can tell that Matthew isn't biting on her bait, "Oh, will you give me a massage? Please! I'm so tense right now." She pleads.

He tries to resist, but his feet push him forward and before he knows it he is in her house. She closes the door behind her and locks it. She grabs Matthew's neck and pulls him close. She breathes on his neck and sighs. "I am surrounded by plastic fake people all the time. It's so nice to meet a real man." She puts her lips on Matthew's mouth and starts to kiss him. He kisses her back.

"Wow! It's been a very long time for me since I kissed a girl. This is all happening so fast." Matthew is hypnotized. "I should probably go. I'm sure you have a busy day ahead of you."

"I have nothing to do today except you." Jade smiles. She starts to take her shirt off. Matthew looks away. Jade grabs his face and turns it back towards her. "What? You can look. I know you have seen my body before. It's everywhere. Everyone has seen it. What's the big deal?"

Matthew looks up, "You don't even know me. Why would you be the least bit interested in me? None of this even makes sense. Maybe we could take it a lot slower. You know, get to know each other first."

Jade laughs, "I know you plenty already. Right now I just want you upstairs with me. Let's go have some fun. Don't you think I'm pretty?"

Matthew gets even more nervous, "Oh man, you don't know how much I've wanted to hear someone say that to me for such a long time. There is something very wrong with me for saying this, but I'm going to have to politely decline your offer." He reaches for the door "I would be happy to talk with you if I can help you in some way."

"You can help me in some way. Let's go upstairs." She says with a pouty look.

"Yeah, I...I think I love someone else actually." Matthew stutters.

"Then why are you here with me? Why did you lead me on and waste my time and let me kiss you? Who is she? Your ex?" Jade becomes irritable.

"No. We never actually went out. I helped her brother. He was getting mugged and I kind of saved his life." Matthew says as he hangs his head.

"So you never even went out with this Lacey girl and you think she loves you back? Give me a break. She probably doesn't even remember you! That was months ago. Come upstairs with me." Jade snaps back as she starts taking her pants off.

Jade is very sexy. Matthew is trying not to stare at her body. It is even better in real life than in her ads. She has smooth skin and curves in all the right places. "Wait? How did you know her name? I never told you that did I? And how did you know that it was months ago?"

"Who cares about that girl anyway? She is yesterday's news. I am today's headline. I am standing here practically naked right in front of you. Every guy in the world is shaking his head right now wondering what is the matter with you." She steps closer to Matthew and puts her arms around his neck again. She starts kissing his neck. She grabs his arms and puts them around her waist. "I know I turn you on. I can tell." She smiles and looks down.

Matthew closes his eyes and asks for guidance. "Am I ruining a good thing right now? Maybe she is the one? I'm trying to do the right thing, but she is making it so hard. I mean so difficult. Please if this isn't right show me a sign." Jade moves his hands down lower. She starts kissing his mouth.

6 That Seems Odd

Matthew and Jade have moved to the couch and they are kissing. Matthew is very conflicted but also very tempted. Jade is on top of him. She starts taking his shirt off. Matthew's phone keeps getting text messages, but he keeps ignoring them. Jade whispers, "Can you please turn that thing off? It is distracting. Better yet give me your number. You'll like this," She types in his number and takes her bra off. She takes several pictures of herself and sends them to him. "That last text is from me. Take a look."

Matthew reaches in his pocket and pulls out his phone, but it takes his breath away when he sees who the texts are from. Lacey has been texting him. Jade assumes he is staring at her pictures and so she sits back smugly smiling to herself. The texts say:

"I don't know if you remember me. My name is Lacey. You saved my brother's life. My brother Stephen (since you probably save a lot of lives). I made you dinner and I thought we had a real connection. I never heard from you again. I'm sure I must have done something wrong or maybe I wasn't good enough for you so I haven't bothered you, but I need your help. Stephen wasn't here when I came back from work a few days ago. I have looked everywhere for him, but I am worried."

"Obviously, this isn't your responsibility and I'm sorry for even asking. I know you really made a huge impact on his life. You seemed like such a beautiful soul. I just don't know who else to turn to."

"Never mind. I'm sorry I even asked. I'm sure you are a busy man and don't even remember me."

"I don't know why I said that. That was petty. If you could call me I would really appreciate it. I'm really worried about him."

"And it would be nice to see you too."

"Pretty hot, huh babe?" Jade smirked.

"What? Oh, yeah." Matthew starts to put his shirt back on. "Hey look, I'm sorry. I have to go. Something just came up. It was really nice meeting you."

"What!" Jade screeches, "Nobody leaves me. Who do you think you are? You are some nobody from a coffee shop. And you don't even drink coffee. You are a loser!" She yells after him as he goes toward the door.

"You are probably right. I shouldn't have come here. I'm really sorry." Matthew says under his breath as he texts Lacey back:

"I'm sorry. I couldn't get to my phone. Where are you? I will come right now."

"Babe. I'm sorry. I didn't mean that. You are a sweetheart. Come lay back down with me." Jade pleads.

Matthew's phone gets another text from Lacey:

"I'm at my house. Do you remember where that is or should I send you the address?"

Matthew doesn't even acknowledge Jade. He just replies to the text:

"I know where it is. I'm on my way."

"Babe! Look at me! Where are you going? You can't walk away from me. Do you know who I am? I am the face of beauty and the voice of the people. When I glance in your direction you take notice and listen!" Jade yells at him as he walks out the door.

Matthew closes the door behind him and then realizes what he has done. He opens the door back up slightly and says, "I had a great time. It was nice meeting you."

"You will regret this. You are making a huge mistake!" Jade yells.

As Matthew walks to the end of the street he notices a sticker on a stop sign that says "No Regrets." He snickers to himself. "What are the odds of that?"

He immediately starts to feel better once he leaves Jade's house. It is like a huge weight has been lifted off him. He is pretty ashamed of himself for letting it get that far that quick, but he is also very excited to get another chance to see Lacey.

The more he thinks about it he doesn't want to be with a girl like Jade anyway. Sure it sounds good in theory, but the reality of it was unsettling and borderline scary. It was as if she had him in a trance. Like most men Matthew has issues with lust. He wished he didn't, but if he was being honest it was his biggest weakness. She knew right where to hit him too.

She was like a professional. She just captivated him from the first glance and offered him everything he ever wanted boldly in full view of everyone with her eyes wide open. She wasn't the least bit shy. He needed to get her out of his mind since he was about to see Lacey. It was time to put his mind on more important things, things that really mattered.

He wonders how cheaters even do it. "This is so stressful" he thought. "An hour ago I was just going for a run wondering what to do with my day. I was a single guy with no hope of meeting anyone. And now I feel like I am cheating on someone I only met one time with someone I met this morning while I was trying to get water. It is really messing with my head." He tries to shake it off and just focus on helping Lacey with her dilemma, but he is legitimately excited to get to see her again.

He finally arrives at her house and rings the doorbell. She answers immediately. She is a real beauty. There is nothing fake about Lacey. She looks so happy to see him. She hugs Matthew and holds on tightly. Matthew hugs her back. They hold each other for a very long time. Neither one wants to let go. The door swings open a little and Stephen walks by. He has cut his hair and shaved his face. He looks healed from the beating. He looks very sane and put together. Matthew lets go of Lacey.

"Is that Stephen? But I thought?" Matthew is confused.

"He came home right after you texted me, but I still wanted to see you. Is that ok?" Lacey says sheepishly.

"Yes, of course. I have wanted to see you since the last time I was here, but I thought you wouldn't want to." Matthew admits.

"Why would you think that? We had such a great time together. Why didn't you call me? You know what it doesn't matter. You are here now. It's nice to see you. Come inside." Lacey gestures him toward the couch.

As the conversation went on day turned into night. Matthew and Lacey spent every day together from that point forward. They loved and respected each other very much. They shared each other's burdens. It was really exciting to watch and be a part of. Secretly Matthew felt like he had dodged a bullet with Jade and almost lost a real treasure with Lacey.

He was so very grateful for her. It felt like she completed him. She was the missing puzzle piece that he had been looking for. She supported him in all his work. She was inspired by how he wanted to make the world a better place. She said all the time how it made her want to be a better person too just watching him. She had amazing insight and always seemed to know just the right things to do and say to lift his spirit and keep him on the right path. They became best friends. Matthew got to the point where he couldn't imagine his life without her.

One night while they were eating dinner she let it slip that she knew about Jade and that's why she had texted him so desperately that day. At first Matthew just dismissed this information, but it began to gnaw away at him. Not the fact that she knew, he would have told her. But he was sure he hadn't told her and so he wondered how she knew.

He had never told anyone about that morning with Jade. In fact he had been alone that entire morning until he ran into Jade. And then he went straight from Jade's house to Lacey's house without telling anyone or seeing anyone that he knew. He racked his brain trying to figure out how she could have known that. It really began to bother him. He replayed the whole scenario in his head over and over again.

There were some pretty weird signs that morning too now that he thought about it. What are the odds of all those things lining up that morning? The massage billboard with Jade on it could be dismissed because her face was everywhere. But what was the likelihood that he would notice that particular billboard out of all the other billboards that morning?

Ok, she was a half-naked girl. Those usually grab his attention even in a cluttered landscape. But then what about finding the free massage coupon face up right after that? And his phone ringing right before he got to the trash can so he was distracted and kept it in his pocket?

What about the coffee shop being the only place around when he was thirsty? And even though he was going to keep walking they had a sign for water... at a coffee shop! And then Jade happened to be there and he happened to bump into her and she wanted him to walk her home.

And when he asked for a sign as to whether or not he should stay with Jade his phone started ringing almost instantly with messages from Lacey, even though he ignored them at first. Was this a huge amount of coincidences?

Was he overthinking this situation? He didn't know. He did know that it was pretty suspicious. But why? Why would all these things happen? Who would even care enough to orchestrate such an elaborate plan? And what would they be trying to get out of him anyway? What would be the point? What was the end game? Who really cares who Matthew Jacobs has as a girlfriend?

He didn't have any real money to speak of. He wasn't famous or well known. He volunteered at a homeless shelter and tried to help people when he could. He used to make decent money, but he didn't really work like he used to. Somehow all his needs were met though. He felt like that was some kind of miracle in itself. He would look and there wouldn't be enough and he would look again and somehow there was enough. He couldn't think of a solution that made sense so he dismissed it as pure happenstance. But he still kept it in the back of his mind because something just didn't feel right.

He started to try to look for more signs in his everyday life. He wanted to test this theory. He wanted to know if somehow someone actually cared about the decisions he made in his life. Why would they? He wasn't anything special. Clearly there had been signs in his life that were impossible to explain without outside intervention. Suddenly he wanted to know more about whoever was intervening in his life and why. He was grateful. Of that there was no doubt. He was also curious.

He brought it up to Lacey a few days later and she tried to avoid the questions for a while. Finally she broke down and said she saw something about it on a gossip magazine's website. That satisfied him for a minute but the more he thought about it the more that didn't make sense either. What are the odds of that? Yes, a few people took pictures of Jade while they were walking home but could that have made it into gossip news that fast?

And who would care about him? He started to ask more questions until Lacey asked, "Do you want me to show you the article? Would that make you happy?" Matthew did want to see the article so she looked quickly on her phone to find it. Her phone rang almost immediately. She answered it and said to Matthew, "I have an emergency. I have to go right now. I'll show you when I get back." Matthew let her go. It was a legitimate call, although conveniently timed for sure.

Later that night Lacey invited Matthew to dinner at her house. She was very sweet to him and made his favorite meal. They ate and they talked but Lacey never brought up the article. After the kitchen was cleaned and everything was put away Matthew asked if she wouldn't mind looking for that article. She immediately pulled it up on her phone. "Oh yeah, here it is. Sorry I forgot to show you."

As she had described the article had pictures of Matthew and Jade walking to her house. It had pictures of her holding his arm and pulling him in the house. The headline said, "Who is the new man in Jade's life?" The date was right and everything that Lacey had said was in the article. It even said that he had left abruptly shortly after going inside.

"That must have been painful for you. I'm so sorry. It was a moment of weakness. I'm so happy I found you instead of her." Matthew apologized.

Lacey looks down sadly and then looks back up at him. "It was difficult but that is when I knew I couldn't wait any longer. If I wanted to have you I had to reach out to you first. I'm really glad you never did anything with her. I'm really glad you are with me." Her eyes filled with tears and she kissed Matthew and then hugged him for a long time. "It was so hard to watch you with her. I couldn't stop myself. I just love you so much Matthew."

"You have always felt like home to me Lacey. I can't explain it. From the first time I saw you I felt like you were the one for me. It broke my heart to be away from you. I thought about you the whole time I was with her." Matthew stopped himself, "That didn't sound good at all. I was never with her. I'm going to shut up right now."

"I know you weren't Matthew. I know." Lacey whispers, "It's not your fault, but it was a pretty close call. I almost lost you."

"You couldn't have lost me. I had only met you once..." Matthew scoffed.

She put her hand over Matthew's mouth, "Shhhhhh, don't say anything else. It isn't helping. Trust me. Let this one go."

7 The Truth

The next day Matthew just couldn't get all of this out of his mind. He talked to everyone he met about it. People at the shelter heard his theories. He asked random questions to people on the street. Cashiers, friends, acquaintances, nobody could get near him without some deep conversations about all the coincidences he was experiencing.

He didn't know how to explain it. He didn't have answers. He wanted answers. Nobody else seemed to have them either. As soon as it seemed like a conversation was getting somewhere something or someone would come and interrupt. It was so frustrating for him. He sat on a bench with his head in his hands and mumbled to himself, "I just want to know the truth. Is that too much to ask?"

Right then a man ran up out of nowhere and sat down next to Matthew. No one else was around. He looked around nervously. Matthew looked uncomfortable.

"Hey brother. Look. I don't have much time and I shouldn't be telling you this but I'm about to blow your mind. Are you ready?" Matthew nods slowly "Never mind. Nothing can prepare you for what you are about to hear. Look around. None of this is real. You are playing a game right now and the entire world is glued to their television sets watching how it will play out. You are the star. Matthew Jacobs is at the center of every conversation in the world right now.

Everything you experience is orchestrated to discover if you will make the right choices. It is very difficult to do, but not impossible. In fact you are doing really well. Much better than any of us thought you would do. Record-breaking, world changing kind of stuff if you must know.

Some very important people are not happy with your success. Do you follow what I'm saying? You are in trouble man. Things are about to get really difficult for you, but you have to stay strong. Just keep following the signs. This will all be over soon."

Matthew is confused, "I literally have no idea what you are talking about. Who are you?"

"I'm sorry let me start over. My name is Tom. I am on your team. Well, technically speaking I am part of your conscience. Do you understand what I'm saying?" Tom is talking at a very fast pace and looking around in a panic.

"I can tell by the look on your face that you have no idea what I'm talking about. This is so weird. On the outside world we hang out all the time. They have you all dumbed down in here. Ok. Let me rewind some more. Are you familiar with the hit virtual reality TV game show called The Hard Road?"

"Never heard of it. I don't watch much TV. How do you have a virtual reality game show? That doesn't even make sense." Matthew replies.

"Right. Of course you don't remember. They wiped your memory up to a certain point. Ok. Look. You signed up to be a contestant on the show. I'm assuming you can't remember..." He looks at the blank stare on Matthew' face,

"...no. You cant. Do you remember your last video gig? The one where Sleek Zeke spoke? There was a guy who was blindfolded and he had to walk a path of good and evil. Well, that was your splice. Before that was real life, but since then you have been living inside your head for months. Well, not exactly inside your head really. Your body is in a deep sleep hooked to an interactive machine that responds to all your body's movements and your mind is jacked into something similar to the Matrix. Are you following me so far? Does any of this sound familiar to you?"

Matthew laughs "Seriously, who put you up to this? This is classic. Is my birthday coming up? No, it's not for 4 months. What is this for? Lacey did this didn't she? I love her." He looks around for cameras or people laughing, but he notices that all the streets are empty. Cars are driving by occasionally, but there are no people anywhere. It is eerie.

"Yeah, you noticed. No people. I bought you ten minutes without distractions. It cost my entire budget so listen up because this is important. When Zeke did that whole demonstration he was explaining the rules to the game. Sorry, Zeke is the host of your show. When he said there was no show without you he meant it. The difference between his game and the one you are playing is that in this game there isn't just one conscience that you can hear. There is a team of us that collectively are your conscience.

We have very strict rules that we have to follow though. We have a very small budget to buy media: billboards, signs, radio ads, social media promotions, TV ads although they are way out of our budget and you don't watch much TV anyway. We can't tell you a lot of things. You have to figure them out on your own.

We can give you clues and signs. Typically you have to choose something that nobody in their right mind would choose for us to be able to unlock a clue for you for your next move. Taking a beating for a hobo, quitting a lucrative career, turning down a super model, paying for a burned down house. I mean dude! You have been nailing it."

"Wait. What? How do you know about any of that stuff? I never told anyone about any of those things." Matthew is very confused.

"Are you even listening to me?" Tom pokes Matthew in the head several times with his finger aggressively, "Hear the words that are coming out of my mouth man! This is a game. You have to accomplish ten good deeds and do ten good things before your time runs out. You have to avoid the bad things and stay on course. If you do both you and your conscience team will split one billion dollars! That is one thousand million dollars! That is a lot of money.

If not the other team gets the money. The stakes are very high. Literally the entire world is invested in this show. This is serious life changing stuff here man!"

"Does the other team have rules too?" Matthew asks, "I mean assuming what you are saying is true."

"Yeah they have rules. They can do and say almost anything they want. They have full control of the media and almost all the population. They have unlimited budgets. They can litter your entire life with a blanket of distractions with no recourse whatsoever. They can't physically force you to do the wrong thing, but everything just short of that is fair game.

They can lie, tell the truth, beg, plead, reason with, have elaborate schemes or conspiracy theories, or any means they can imagine or create. And here is the kicker. You don't have to do bad things to lose. All they have to do is get you off course so you don't do the good things on your list before the time runs out.

The odds are stacked against you brother. And the bad guys are not happy with your progress let me tell you. You are close, real close to winning this game. You are about to blow this whole thing out of the water if they can't stop you. And we are talking about a huge amount of money.

They aren't going to let that happen without a fight. You've got to watch your back. Stay on the straight and narrow. Finish this thing. We are counting on you. Do you understand? I've got to go. My time is almost up."

Matthew just sits there with his jaw dropped open trying to process all of this.

"So, is the real world like this? How will I know the difference? Is Lacey real?" Matthew asks.

"Yeah, she is your wife in real life. That is why it hurt her so bad to see you with Jade. I mean she understands don't get me wrong. She is on our team for sure. She was your reward for saving Stephen. Have you noticed how much she encourages you to do the right thing? Have you noticed how supportive she is? Real girls aren't like that. She is one of us." Tom reaffirms.

"Is that why I was attracted to her right away and felt drawn to her like I did?" Matthew asks.

"Probably, we are on the cutting edge with all of this stuff. We don't fully understand what we are doing. I think the producers are working for someone to be honest with you. Someone huge!" Tom continues.

"Like CBS?" Matthew asks.

"No man, like controllers of the world. People out there are changing because of you. People have hope. They are actually being kind to each other. I don't know if this kind of thing has ever really happened to be honest. People want to be like you. They are seeing the fruit of your labor and they are inspired to be like you.

It's like when you succeed the rest of the world does to, but when you fail...if you fail you may just kick the wind out of any goodness that is left in humanity. So don't! No pressure, but seriously don't." Tom says very seriously.

"So, how is it that you are telling me all this? Shouldn't that be against the rules? I mean if I know I am playing a game then I will act differently right?" Matthew asks earnestly.

Tom tries to defend himself, "Yeah. I know. I really shouldn't be telling you any of this. It is a grey area in the rules."

Matthew is still confused, "But why are you telling me this? If I really were winning then why would you intervene? If you really were on my team why wouldn't you let me play the game with integrity? Isn't that what a conscience does? If I am supposed to take the hard road why are you trying to make it easy for me? If I win I want to earn it.

I'm not a coward and I'm not a cheater. Why would you tell me any of this? I still don't know if any of what you are saying is even true. I just can't imagine that you have my best interest at heart no matter how you slice it."

Tom hangs his head, "Because you asked? I was just trying to help you understand. We are friends."

"TOM!" a loud voice calls from across the street. Zeke stands sternly and then starts marching across the street with great intention, "GO! NOW!" He points his finger at Tom and then to his right. Tom tries to explain for a moment, but Zeke cuts him off, "You! Leave now!"

Tom looks back apologetically at Matthew and then steps in front of a bus that runs him over. Zeke turns Matthew around and starts walking him in the other direction "Don't look at him. He is gone now."

Matthew is in shock, "Did he? Did he just kill himself?"

Zeke brushes it off like it's nothing, "No. Well, yes, but...it's hard to explain. Look Tom shouldn't have told you any of that. It is blatantly against the rules. Our judges were on lunch break and he locked himself in and everyone else out while he came and destroyed what we have all worked so hard for.

He is a part of your conscience team and because of what he just did you have been disqualified. I'm sorry. Your game is over. The judges have spoken. I've got nothing for you. You can hang out here. Enjoy yourself. It will take a while to finish up the paperwork and get you out, until then it doesn't really matter what you do.

We are turning off the live feed. We are basically just running out the clock. Suddenly and without warning you will just wake up and all this will be a memory. I'm sorry Matthew. You were very close. You had a good run. You will still get some nice parting gifts from our sponsors just for participating. Good game."

"Wait, but...I didn't know. I didn't ask him to do that. This isn't my fault." Matthew tries to plead with Zeke.

"Your fates are tied together remember? You are part of a team. Your team failed. Accept it. Be a good loser. Take a knee. Go sit on the bench and run out the clock. See you on the other side kid. Maybe we can get lunch sometime and talk about it." Zeke says smugly.

He takes off his wig and rips off his mustache as he walks away. He unbuttons his shirt and lets his belly flop out. He closes his eyes and takes a deep breath, "I always hate this part." Zeke walks towards the curb. "Remember if you can't take it and you want to come home sooner you end the game like this. And here is how it's done kid. You can't think about it." He steps in front of a truck. The truck can't stop in time. Matthew turns his head away. He closes his eyes. He hears a loud crack and tires screeching. But when he opens his eyes Zeke has just disappeared.

8 Commentary

"And there you have it folks. It seems like all hope is lost for Matthew Jacobs. What a tragic end to such an inspiring story. But don't go anywhere. We have a real surprise coming up for you. But first, let's review his journey so far. Ted?"

"Thanks Janice. Matthew Jacobs, a video technician from Middle America, was told by a friend that he should try out for our show. We were looking for someone with integrity and strength of character that could walk The Hard Road. We wanted someone who was willing to let the entire world see his every move, his every breath, and his every thought. To test him and see if he really had what it took to navigate through a moral gauntlet and come out unscathed."

"And Ted we are so glad he said yes. Right now as you all know we are nine months into his one-year time limit to complete the ten good deeds and achieve the title of Victor! Matthew has proven to be a worthy competitor indeed. And he is so entertaining. The Hard Road is broadcast in 190 countries worldwide. It has the largest staff and budget of any production in history. Let's review his progress so far, but first let's take a look at the teams that make all this possible."

"On the Conscience Team we have 4 players. Matthew's wife in real life works as an executive assistant for an oil company. She makes a modest salary, but has always dreamed of more. By her own admission their marriage wasn't fantastic before the show begun. These two have become a seemingly unstoppable force. Ladies and gentleman give it up for (in a booming voice) Lacey Jacobs (applause).

Lacey was unlocked a little late in the game but has made quite an impact since her arrival. The game was originally designed for the spouse to be introduced much earlier in the game and allowed to be a sounding board for all the decisions that needed to be made. She can't make the final call, but she is a necessary support system in an often-confusing world.

Who can forget the agony that she felt when Jade took Matthew to her house and almost seduced him? What a tear jerker" Ted wipes a tear from his eye, "I can't imagine how difficult that must have been for her. If I ever saw my wife Trudy with someone else I just don't know what I would do. But Lacey fought for her man and she got him back. Better late then never."

"I love my husband and I believe in him. I think we have fallen more in love since the show began then we have in all the years we were married before The Hard Road. He was gone a lot before the show. He worked out of town a lot is what I mean. He has really blossomed and I am so happy to get to be a part of it. I'm so proud of the man he has become." Lacey says as she looks up from her monitors. She looks very intense as she looks back at her screens. She is clearly in the middle of an important battle and doesn't want to be distracted.

"Handling Defense and Encouragement we have Matthew's best friend since the second grade. He always keeps his head in the game. He is a relentless force of brotherly love. He blocks many of the attacks that Matthew never even sees coming. A man any of us would love to have on our team (in a booming voice) Noah Tallman (thunderous applause).

You probably remember Noah from the beginning of the season when he was the conscience at Matthew's training ceremony. He wears many different faces and uses all the tools at his disposal to make sure that Matthew is protected on all sides and that he has the inner strength to carry on through the many perils that the enemy throws their way. Who can forget the months that Noah spent as Matthew's friend and mentor Evan Joshua? The heartbreak that accompanied the house burning down was one of the first huge landmarks in his journey."

"I had to sell it so that he believed me. I knew the house would burn down before we ever started working on the house. We all did. But of course I couldn't let on. That would be against the rules. He had to see the tragedy and offer to help. That was really the only thing he had to do.

Had he not offered up his own money I would have magically found some as long as he just offered to help me in a hard situation we could move forward. It took my breath away when he offered his own money. He risked everything for me. He had skin in the game for sure. The money he was giving wasn't real, but he didn't know that.

It was a huge sacrifice on his part. I had no idea that he had such a kind heart. You would think you know someone after being friends for all these years. Those tears you saw were real. Working with Matthew has made me want to be a better human being. I think he has had that effect on everyone. We just had no idea how good he would do at this." Noah holds his head a little higher the more he talks. You can tell how proud he is of Matthew.

"On Offense and Exhortation we have Matthew's father in real life. A pillar of strength and stability to his son he is what every father hopes to aspire to one day. He is the incarnation of a loving protector with the heart of a lion. Matthew grew up calling him dad, but we know him as (in a booming voice) David Jacobs (applause with standing ovation).

David is always looking for ways to push his son to the next level. He knows how important this game is and it is his job to keep the next goal at the forefront of Matthew's mind. David organized the awareness rally in front of Matthew's window within seconds of his decision to ask for help at the beginning of the game. Of course this led to Matthew changing careers and helping Evan with the flip house.

He also stood beside his son as he was beaten by thugs in an alley and offered strength and encouragement to stand in the face of adversity for what was right."

Wiping away tears, "That was so very hard for me to watch. I love my son and I have always been proud of him, but wow what he did that day was unbelievable. What a hero! He was willing to give his life for a total stranger. A father couldn't be prouder of his son than I was that day. I don't even care if we win or lose. That is my son." He fights back tears "That is my son" sniff "And I love him!"

"And rounding off the conscience team is Matthew's younger brother in real life. He has a computer engineering degree with a minor in business. He is as fast on his digital feet as he is creative. He knows what will get Matthew's attention and tries to stay ahead of the eight ball. He says that his youth group is praying for him every day to be aware of the enemy at every turn so that he can protect and guide his brother. Folks we all need a brother like this guy (booming voice) Peter Jacobs (applause).

Peter is in charge of all media and tech. It is Peter's job to place 'arrows' along the path to guide Matthew in the right direction. This is no easy task. He is given a very sparse advertising budget with very strict rules about what he can and cannot say in his media ads. His time limits are usually very short. He arranged the signs at the parade and the 'No Regrets' sticker on the stop sign as he left Jade's house. You probably don't notice most of his work. Matthew walks right by a lot of it without giving it a second thought. But I guess if he knew it was his brother he might pay more attention."

Peter pushes his glasses back towards his eyes as he looks up from his computer screen. He is a little cross-eyed and quirky, "I try to look ahead at the game and predict what kind of media will get Matthew's attention. I have to make most of it long before he actually needs it. As you all know the game is very fluid so it changes constantly. You have to roll with it. I'm not very good at this whole thing to be honest. I feel like I am chasing my own tail most days.

When he actually sees and acknowledges and acts on a message I have sent him it is an amazing connection though I've got to say. That 'No Regrets' sticker was a last minute throw together but it really hammered the message home. I was like go be with your wife already brother. Get away from that skank. I was like yes!!! Finally he gets it!" Peter stands up quickly and his headphones pull him back to his chair "Sorry, I get a little excited about this stuff."

"And now for the opposing team 'Doubt and Chaos'. We have assembled an all-star team of life-long deceivers. These folks play mean and dirty. They are ruthless. The only thing they love more than money, fame and power is ruining lives. They will stop at nothing to not only win the prize money but to utterly destroy Matthew. Let's take a look at the players.

On False Signs and Wonders, a defense attorney from New York, you might remember her as the lawyer that ended free internet and fought for industrial rights to dump toxic waste that eventually led to poisoning the city of Welimded, Florida killing 2,318 people and bringing the American alligator into extinction. She also brought a case to the Supreme Court that exonerated Hitler for any war crimes he may have allegedly committed during World War 2. There is no doubt that she gets bad things done in a hurry. The Beast from the East, The Liar from the Fire, Hell's Daughter for the Slaughter (in a booming voice) Sue Dough (reluctant applause).

Sue's main focus on the team is to arrange for convincing signs that lead Matthew off track. No doubt this is a difficult task as Matthew has a strong conscience that isn't easily swayed. Now for some of Sue's highlights from the game. Sue arranged for the free massage coupon to be at Matthew's feet at just the right time. She brought his attention to the Rehydrate sign at the coffee shop. She pushed him along the path to Jade's house and almost succeeded in ruining his marriage and leaving him spouseless for the entirety of his game.

This would have been a heavy blow to Matthew and his game. It is almost impossible to get through this maze alone. Sue knows how important it is to destroy families and marriages. In spite of her failures she continues to chip away at the marriage in any little way she can. She is constantly searching for any chink in the armor that she can pry her way into.

Although she hasn't succeeded yet she is hoping to start a fight between Matthew and Lacey right before bedtime and hopes to have them go to sleep angry at each other. This will plant a seed that can grow into resentment, fights, and hopefully divorce or better yet infidelity.

Sue has also had some real flops. Like when she had the police break up the Awareness Parade. As you all know it just further validated Matthew as he moved forward in the game."

Sue looks up from her computer screens and smiles slowly, "You better believe I have Matthew's attention now. I'm about to unleash the beast on him. Every bad thing that comes his way is going to be validated with signs and wonders. We are about to pull out all the stops. Fans are going to love this next few months Ted. I have been working on some pretty crafty deceptions and I think you will be shocked at what comes next. Stay tuned."

"On The Media Circus we have a Hollywood producer responsible for over 51 movies, 17 TV shows and get this over 13,000 commercials! He is a virtual media machine! He wanted to produce this show but thank God there are conflict of interest laws that won't allow it. This player doesn't need the money. He just wants more. He is known for being a cutthroat businessman in his industry. He has lots of people around him, but by his own admission he has no real friends. The Prince and Power of The Air, The Great Deceiver, The Lord of Illusions (in a booming voice) MediaM (thunderous applause).

In the game and in real life he controls TV, radio, Internet, and almost all advertising. He literally shapes the landscape of the world we see every day. He shapes thoughts and sways whole nations whichever direction will keep Matthew from finishing the race.

Probably one of Matthew's worst enemies, MediaM has been crusading a never-ending assault on Matthew's sub-conscious since the moment he began this game. He openly mocks the decisions that could advance Matthew in the game. He misdirects and distracts and misinforms constantly everywhere Matthew turns. I don't know how he does it folks. I doubt if he has slept since the game began."

MediaM has wild eyes, "You asked if I ever sleep? Sure, I do. Sometimes my eyes close when I sneeze. I don't have time to sleep." He rubs his gums with his finger and twitches, "I can sleep when Matthew is dead. The stakes are too high. I will wear him down bit by bit. Just like a river cutting through the Grand Canyon I am digging paths in his mind that seem shallow and harmless until they are too deep to climb out of. He won't even know he is making the wrong decisions. I will hypnotize him with a nonstop neon hum that will numb his mind and his soul and leave him utterly worthless in this game.

His absolute annihilation is what keeps me up at night. The hope that I will ruin him and make myself filthy rich in the process is euphoric to me. It's like a drug. I don't want to leave one single place in his entire world where he can avoid my influence. I want to own him 24/7. One day when all this is over I am going to meet him in the real world. Our eyes will lock and though he doesn't know my face he will know that he is mine. He will recognize my voice. This is my calling. This. Is. Why. I. Was. Boooorn!" He stares intensely at the camera for an awkwardly long time.

"OK? And on Temptation is a man responsible for over 83% of the porn on the Internet. If you use a dating app chances are he has something to do with it. He also has umbrella companies that produce gossip and fashion magazines. You don't know his name, but you know his work, trust me. Ladies and Gentlemen The Temptation of the Nations, The Darkness Within, The Bold Faced Lie, (in a booming voice) Venomous Itch (hesitant applause).

He screamed in Matthew' ear to run away during the famous mugging where Matthew was willing to die. He was the one who offered Matthew drugs backstage during the strike. Matthew almost fell on his first night in the game. He was the voice that prompted Matthew to hurt or kill the homeless girl in Evan's flip house. Probably his most famous move thus far has been Jade. (tugs collar and looks off camera) That was some steamy stuff let me tell you."

Itch snaps his fingers, "That Jade scene was seeeeeeexy though, wasn't it? MmmHmm I could eat that boy up. When I win this game I'm going to look him up and let him earn some of that money back he lost. Lacey is going to have to share that man with me. And you better believe Jade isn't out of this game yet. I'm going to find cracks in his marriage and the moment I do Jade will be there with arms wide open to take him back and ease the pain. I've got some other tricks up my sleeve that I have been working on too. Keep watching and vote for me as your MVP on social media." Itch blows a kiss to the camera.

"And last but not least on Distraction and Diversion we have a CIA operative who is a master of deceit. We aren't allowed to show his face or voice because he is involved in several ongoing investigations (under his breath) and some wet work I am told. Just trust us when we say this guy has been involved in some ruthless takeovers and massive deceptions through his many years of service. This guy could kill you 23 different ways just by looking at you. The Psychological Killer, The Compassion Assassin, The Hand of the Devil, all the way from an undisclosed location (in a booming voice) FrienZee (frenzied applause).

FrienZee seemed to be a strong contender at the beginning of this game but he has been taking a beating for months now. Matthew just doesn't seem to allow any distractions in his life. He stays laser focused and on task. It is almost impossible to sway him. He doesn't look to the left or to the right. He stays on the straight and narrow. But there may be a plan in place to shake Matthew's whole game."

Frienzee appears as a shadow with a garbled voice. He starts bragging, "That Tom character was 100% my idea. It is a big risk telling Matthew he is in the game. Of course his conscience would never be allowed to tell him that, but we aren't constrained by such restrictive rules.

So, the thought was that we tell him he is in the game but immediately tell him he is disqualified from the game and that he should just give up and enjoy himself while he rides out the clock. I think fans of the show are going to love this twist. It's genius really. If we can just get him to feel that what he does isn't important than I think we have a chance of winning.

And pretending to have Zeke kill himself like that was probably one of my most amazing deceptions of all. My plan is to first plant this suicide seed in him and then water it every chance we get. If he is actually stupid enough to kill himself we get twice the money. But even if he doesn't go through with it we can bring a dark depression over him that will distract him from his final tasks and we may be able to pull a victory out of this after all.

I'm going to be honest with you the fact that we kept him away from Lacey for so long was monumental for us. And when we almost had him sleep with Jade we could taste the victory. We knew it was just a matter of time. But once we lost him to Lacey it has been hopeless. It is an uphill battle that we feel like we can't even win. Most days we barely put in any real effort because we know it won't do any good anyway. But this new move is about to change everything for us. I feel very hopeful about our future. In my mind I have already started spending my prize money. It's close. I might even retire, probably not. I love hating what I do."

9 Let's Review

Janice the Announcer cuts back in, "I told you that surprise was worth waiting for. How exciting folks! It appeared like Tom was sent from the Conscience Team. It looked like Matthew's game was over because his team members had betrayed him and broken the rules of the game. It seemed like all hope was lost. Believe me I was right there with you folks. I almost thought I was out of a job." Janice wipes her brow nervously, "It was like having the rug pulled out from under me. A lot of you probably didn't know what to do with yourselves when you saw this. It literally took my breath away!"

Ted chimes in, "Yeah Janice you screamed when Tom started spilling the beans. We can only see the feed that you guys see so we didn't know who was behind it. This has been one of the biggest plot twists I could have ever possibly imagined."

Janice cuts him off, "Ted I had no idea that suicide clause was somewhere in the fine print. You have to hand it to FrienZee. He really does his homework. I'm glad he doesn't work for our country's enemies. We would be in trouble."

Ted shakes his head, "We certainly wouldn't be a super power any more that's for sure. And now to take you through all the current stats and gameplay is our most intelligent commentator Daniel Codey."

Janice chimes in, "Daniel tell us where we are in the game. People are excited to hear the progress."

Motion graphics and upbeat music transition to Daniel Codey in front of a large screen filled with stats and charts that he moves and changes constantly. He hits the ground running with his exciting pace,

"Let's start with the ground rules for any of you that have been living in a hole for the last 9 months. The Hard Road is the first show of it's kind ever. It is a virtual reality game show. We sorted through millions of submissions before choosing Matthew as our contestant. The producers saw a strength of character in him that was unmatched by anyone else we interviewed. He seems so common and everyday, but he has something special inside of him. He has a profound resilience in the face of absolute hopelessness.

His family support system has been a pleasant surprise to everyone too. You can't see the back of your own head. We all need people we can count on. We didn't expect everyone on his side to step up like they have since they are all amateurs and common folk, but wow! Lacey has been so supportive and patient. Noah is a rock of encouragement. David is the father we wish we all had. And Peter is no force to be reckoned with either. Matthew has a small army that he is oblivious to that is screening everything that comes his way to protect him and move him forward in the game.

All right, let's see where we are in the game. I love watching this adventure unfold. Matthew's first task was to do a good deed. He had to inspire someone who had lost hope. His reward if he completed that task and found it was to learn a new trade that he loved. The bad thing he wanted to avoid was developing an addiction. So I'm sure you all were pleasantly surprised by how that turned out.

Matthew was offered drugs backstage after the show and even though he had many sober years he felt compelled to go. The peer pressure was there and Venomous Itch was screaming in his face to take the drugs. But as you know David and Noah stepped in to the circle and encouraged Matthew when he needed it most. Ultimately it was Matthew's decision, but an epic battle was fought that night. Had Matthew taken the drugs he might have still found redemption at some point in the game, but it would have been a major setback. It would have thrown the rest of his game into a tailspin. Ed would have killed himself. In his suicide note he was going to mention how he had completely lost hope in humanity after watching Matthew that night. It would have been devastating. More drugs were waiting for him to help ease the pain and an addiction was imminent. But he weighed the options and chose bravely to not be owned. He probably doesn't even know what a bullet a dodged that night.

And because of this he completed his first good deed. He inspired Ed who had lost hope. He saved a life and got to feel how wonderful that can be. It also led to his opportunity for learning a new trade with Evan. Now he could have turned this down. It didn't seem like a smart choice at the time. But he chose to believe in what he could not see and step out on faith. And look how that turned out. He started down a path that has led him to a joy that is priceless and a life filled with goodness.

Because he completed level one the conscience team was allowed to initiate his next opportunity for a good deed. Their advertising budget increased and they were all encouraged. The opposing team was allowed to pick the setting for the next challenge since they lost the first round. They hadn't given up on the drug addiction option yet. They had hopes for Sharon who had broken into the flip house to somehow introduce drugs into the gameplay and lead Matthew off the path. Had they succeeded Matthew probably would have floundered around aimlessly for the remainder of the game in a daze missing his entire purpose.

Noah, who was posing as Evan at the time, knew that the enemy would be back quickly but he was constrained by a rule that didn't allow him to enter the room until he was summoned. Frienzee started planting seeds in Matthew's mind to murder the intruders. When Matthew resisted he went with the next best thing, inflicting pain. He finally settled for ruining her life, for her own good of course. A plan was in place to tempt Matthew with drugs or sex or provoke him to violence. Any of these would have counted as a victory for Doubt & Chaos.

When Matthew calmed himself and asked for guidance this allowed Evan to enter the room, which he did immediately. Evan commanded the situation. He displayed forgiveness and generosity and kindness that shocked the nations. No one expected that kind of reaction. Technically speaking Matthew hadn't actually helped an enemy. Evan had. That is until Matthew spoke up and offered to call Sharon's parents. This one simple gesture changed the lives of Sharon, her child, her parents, her friends, Evan, Matthew, and honestly the whole world watching.

By doing this he blinded Doubt & Chaos literally. Their feed was nothing but static for 24 hours after that. They still tried to use their weapons, but had no direction or tools to do so. It was as if a blind monkey was just pushing buttons on a machine that he didn't understand. They were rendered powerless by this simple act of kindness. Of course that was Matthew's second good deed, which made him eligible for the opportunity to be healthy. Anyone who has ever been sick can appreciate good health. And so Matthew has enjoyed good health for the duration of the game and has avoided addiction in the process. As you all know once you say no to something it becomes easier and easier to say no to it with each passing time until it has no power over you whatsoever.

As Daniel is talking the audience can see the scenes in Matthew's life that he is talking about. The audience has seen life through Matthew's eyes for the most part, but as this is all being explained the audience is allowed to see behind the curtain. They can see the battles that have gone on behind the scenes to war for Matthew's soul. Although he couldn't see the battles he felt the turmoil and the conflict. And now it was becoming clearer to everyone just what was happening in his soul this whole time. The players disguised as people would show up on screen with angel wings or horns depending on the team they were from. It was interesting to see that many times the villains and angels were not who you would expect them to be.

Matthew's third task was to give away something precious to him. Now we all knew that like most of us Matthew's time is precious to him. He had been a high paid video mercenary so his time and talent was a valuable commodity and he knew it. When the flip house burned down all Matthew was supposed to do was volunteer his time. That would have satisfied the judges and moved him forward in the game unscathed. The bad thing he was avoiding on this move was getting fat. Had he refused to work he had that risk. He could have fallen into inactivity and idleness and gained weight, but instead he shocked us all with what happened next.

He took personal responsibility of this tragedy and put his time and his money at risk. He gave freely with no guarantee of ever being paid back. In fact when Evan offered to write up a contract Matthew refused saying he knew Evan was a man of his word. When we interviewed Noah about this he was in tears. I know I was in tears too. What an impact that made on all of us. Anyone who has ever faced tragedy knows what a blessing someone like Matthew would be. He is like an angel, like a God send. Matthew didn't flinch and he never looked back. He bravely powered through for two months in uncharted territory and came out a victor. Obviously this completed his third good deed. It unlocked the third good blessing, which was the gift of being physically fit. He accomplished this while he worked but it also became his reward.

Fans of the show have asked me privately if it seems right to give him work as a reward so I want to talk about this for a minute because it is a great question. The American dream has changed over the years. It used to be the set of ideals such as democracy, rights, liberty, opportunity and equality in which freedom included the opportunity for prosperity and success, as well as an upward social mobility for the family and children, achieved through hard work in a society with few barriers. In other words people just wanted the opportunity to work and be treated as equals. They wanted the opportunity to operate their own businesses and work hard and be paid for that work.

The American dream has changed through the years. It hasn't changed with fanfare and announcements. It has changed with apathy and complacency and entitlement. Today if you ask the average American what they aspire to it is to get paid a lot of money for doing basically nothing so that they can pay other people to do what they don't want to do. This has escalated to the point that we pay other people to force us to be healthy and lose weight. Today's American dream is literally to do nothing.

But what I am suggesting is that there can be joy in our work. Our work, if we see it as such, is an act of worship. It is a service both to God and our fellow man. And if we have learned nothing from this show let us remember that by helping others we end up helping ourselves along the way. Honestly most of our adult lives will be spent working. Why not do it with your whole heart? Why not be a blessing to those you work with and for? Why not show kindness and mercy to those we do business with? Wouldn't the world be a better place if we would do that?

And so yes, his reward was work. And all the satisfaction that comes with it. He also got the money and the health and the muscles that go with hard work. I hope you are all paying attention because there is a valuable lesson here for all of us. It is not a reward to be able to do nothing. It is a curse and a punishment. I strongly believe that most of our disappointments and frustrations in life come from unrealistic expectations. Moving on.

Matthew's fourth good deed was to turn the other cheek. The bad move he was trying to avoid was getting mugged. Since Doubt & Chaos were on a losing streak they got to choose the terms of the next challenge. After a huddle they came up with this scenario. Matthew wakes up confused in an alley to be a silent witness to a potential murder. Matthew is faced with a very challenging set of choices. None of them seem to have a good outcome.

He could sneak away and pretend he didn't see anything. That would have been an ideal situation for Doubt & Chaos. He would have been seen and then all the aggression would have been shifted to Matthew. They would have mugged him and killed Stephen. This would have opened up a series of events that would have really damaged Matthew and his game. One of the main goals was to make Matthew fear for his life. His life was never in actual danger folks. That was against the rules and all the players knew that.

Venomous Itch crouched next to Matthew behind the dumpster filling his mind with every excuse to leave. He presented every possible outcome with graphic detail and reasoned with Matthew's natural desire for self-preservation. Matthew almost fell for this line of thinking, but his father David appealed to his heart. He pulled out all the stops with arguments about honor and valor and courage. But Itch had a problem for every solution.

He attempted to dehumanize Stephen so that Matthew would feel no pity for him. One for one they presented their arguments to Matthew for consideration. Itch used harsh panicked words that pushed Matthew into a rash decision. David was patient and kind, not trying to force his hand but seeking to lead him in the right direction. Finally David simply asked Matthew what he would want someone to do if they witnessed the same thing happening to him. That was what did it.

Without hesitation Matthew stood up. When he stood up the world sat up a little straighter to watch what would happen? Well by now you already know Matthew showed the world what he was made of; bravery, honor, dignity, courage, integrity and self-sacrifice. He was given every opportunity to run, but he stood firm. When he was punched he fell to the ground and stood back up to take another hit.

What power! What strength that must have taken. Remember folks he doesn't know we are watching him. He doesn't know this is a game and I think that is what is so fascinating. He was willing to give his life that day for an outcast. Nothing slowed him down. His poor father wept beside him as he was beaten and threatened. Here is the actual footage from the scene. You can see David standing between Matthew and the thugs absorbing some of the blows himself for his son. What a beautiful picture of love.

Frienzee was going to take Matthew's money and go through with the mugging even though Matthew had clearly beaten them, but the judges blew the whistle and called a foul. They knew they weren't allowed to kill him and they couldn't mug him unless he tried to resist or run. They were only allowed two punches but when they pistol-whipped Matthew it took the beating too far. Because of this extreme abuse of power they were penalized. In addition to game blindness for the next 24 hours and a secret advantage for Team Conscience they were given bad intelligence for a move later in the game. We can't give details on that, but it will be a game changer.

This is a great time to talk about consequences. Only a fool thinks they can get away with deliberately breaking the rules without their actions having serious consequences. This pattern of taking things too far has become common practice for Doubt & Chaos. It may prove to be the very thing that destroys their game. Time will tell.

So, although it looked like a mugging technically it wasn't because the thugs never took Matthew's belongings. So once again he avoided the pitfall. He made the very best of a very difficulty situation. He showed us what kind of man he is. He completed the fourth good deed by turning the other cheek. And he found the love of his life, which as I'm sure you figured out by now was his reward for this good deed. It was a huge sacrifice, so it was a huge reward. He also completed the fifth good deed, which was to love the unlovely. Stephen, the hobo, just happened to be the brother of Lacey.

I know what you are thinking. But Matthew didn't end up with Lacey until months after that? You are right. Matthew listened to the voice of Doubt and suffered for a long time because of that. He had the reward waiting for him. She was unlocked and in his life waiting patiently, but fear kept him from seeing her. He let himself be blinded by insecurities from his past. Insecurities that weren't even real. In his heart he felt the connection to his wife, but he listened to the wrong voices and lived in loneliness pointlessly. He missed a great support system and more importantly he missed out on the love of his life.

Lacey wasn't allowed to initiate contact with Matthew after he left her house that first night until he reached out to her or until their real life marriage was in jeopardy. Doubt & Chaos were unaware of this rule. None of the players can see the other players. They don't know anything about them except what is revealed during gameplay. They still don't realize that Lacey is Matthew's real life wife. They assume she is a stranger that just wants money and is willing to do anything to get it.

The fifth bad thing Matthew was supposed to avoid was being alone forever. This became a quagmire for Matthew. He believed the lie that he wasn't good enough and that Lacey didn't want to be with him. This one little untruth paralyzed Matthew for months. His character was still strong but he was getting nowhere in the game and time was running out. He did volunteer at the homeless shelter, which was one of his good deeds. He learned some life lessons. He grew stronger in some ways, but he was open to attack by the enemy because of his loneliness.

This eventually led to his temptation with Jade. This was such an emotional string of events. Doubt & Chaos looked like they were finally gaining some real ground. They had been wearing him down for quite some time. Eroding his moral fiber and exhausting him physically with good seeming tasks was all part of the plan.

Then began the onslaught of Jade marketing campaigns. They blanketed the cityscape with her advertisements. They wanted her face and body to be automatically associated with sexual desire. Then they cleared Matthew's schedule for a day. As you know idle hands are the devil's workshop. She went right to work on Matthew from the moment he saw her. Of course Venomous Itch played the role of Jade, which makes it difficult for me to watch now that I know that.

The next pitfall to avoid was getting an STD. Jade has an STD. She has AIDS. That would have been a huge victory for Doubt & Chaos and would have made them a powerful force to be reckoned with while seriously damaging Matthew's chances of ever completing the game. Of course Jade never offered love. She offered meaningless sex. And with it came an unwelcome virus. They only tempted Matthew so they could expose his shame because of how much damage it would do. Matthew almost succumbed to the temptation of Jade, but his conscience reminded him throughout the journey of Lacey and their connection to the point of utter distraction.

When he asked for help and his marriage was in jeopardy this unlocked Lacey to be able to reach out to Matthew, which she did immediately and without veiled intention. She fought for her marriage. She appealed to Matthew's goodness and it worked! Doubt & Chaos had a good foothold, but that was broken almost immediately after Matthew walked out of Jade's house. Shortly after that he claimed his fourth reward of finding the love of his life, which he had unlocked months before. He also defeated his demons of lust and despair, which was his fifth reward. This also completed his sixth good deed, which was to be a friend to someone who desperately needed his friendship. Which in turn led to his sixth reward to live in peace. His reward for volunteering and expecting nothing in return was to be healed of a long-term ailment. That ailment was his loneliness.

This one seemingly simple act set in motion a chain reaction that poured blessings upon Matthew like a waterfall. He checked a lot of things off of his list in a very short amount of time. Make no mistake all these had been building up for quite some time, but potential is not the same as completion. Since Lacey has been by Matthew's side they have been unstoppable. She can see things from far away that Matthew has no idea about. He is oblivious to much of the warfare that goes on around him, but Lacey is a part of it. She guides him away from dangers that he can't even comprehend.

The game has been at a virtual stalemate or so it has seemed for quite some time. Quietly each side has been working towards their next big move. I think the audience has enjoyed watching the love story. It has been inspiring and has encouraged many, but not much has gone on the leaderboard recently. All that is about to change with this latest move though.

What is up the proverbial sleeves of these great rival teams? What is coming up in the final three months of the game? Will Matthew make it across the finish line or will he lose everything he and his team have worked so hard for? I suppose time will tell. One thing is for sure I will be glued to the screen waiting in anticipation to see what happens next.

Matthew has a few challenges left. Let's look at those. On the bad list to avoid are three things: Watch Someone Die, Commit suicide, and Start World War 3. Some have argued that he watched both Tom and fake Zeke die. Others have argued that they didn't actually die they did things that should have killed them and then they disappeared. That will have to be the judge's call.

The three good deeds left on his list are as follows: Forgive the one who has hurt you the worst, Ask forgiveness from the ones you have hurt and do whatever it takes to make it right with them, and Give away everything he has. These are all very difficult goals to achieve for anyone.

If he accomplishes these three last good things then he will unlock his final three rewards which are: Experience true freedom, change the world for the better, and his final reward is to win the lottery.

This has been an exciting adventure so far. I'm sure we will all be eager to see how it turns out. Before we get back to the game we have Zeke, the real Zeke, out in the field to see how you the audience have responded to The Hard Road. I love hearing these stories. Zeke?"

10 The Impact

"Thanks Daniel. The Hard Road is broadcast in 190 countries worldwide. It averages 100 million viewers each week, but we anticipate over 150 million viewers for the season finale. Everyone is crazy about this show. It has made a real impact on the world, far more than we ever could have imagined. It is such an amazing concept. But we had no idea that the players would step up like they have. Doubt & Chaos have proven to be a real powerhouse of deceit and misdirection. They have had some big moves, but when they let the cat out of the bag recently the world stopped turning.

This could completely back fire and ruin their game or it could be the Hail Mary that pulls them across the finish line to victory. It's just hard to say how Matthew will respond to this information. He has surprised us before. FrienZee is very calculated, but he is also very arrogant.

Remember folks their only goal is to make sure that Matthew doesn't complete three more good deeds and claim three more prizes within the next three months. We all know they are hoping for utter destruction or a suicide, which would completely disqualify him and end the game early. It would also double their prize money. But all they have to do to win is keep him away from his goals. Let's hear from some of the fans of darkness."

A larger middle aged man taking garbage to a dumpster behind a restaurant chimes in as he smokes a cigarette, "I love watching how stupid Matthew is sometimes. What an idiot! I would have walked that road in under a month and I would be a billionaire by now. You have to respect Doubt & Chaos though. They are masters at misdirection. Every time he starts getting close to where he should be they just distract him and crush his dreams. Just like real life." As he is dumping the garbage it spills all over him. He just looks at the camera in disgust.

A teenage boy is playing video games in his parents' basement alone, "I don't watch the show that much honestly. But I do love watching people suffer. From what I hear people at school say he suffers a lot so I suppose I wouldn't mind watching that." He reaches for an energy drink but it is empty, "Mom! My drink is empty!"

A very frazzled looking single mom tries to talk to the camera while her children misbehave, "It's just nice to know that I'm not the only person in the world who is in pain right now. Obviously, this is not what I had hoped my life would be like when I grew up. I really always just wanted to be a princess who gets spoiled and told she is beautiful all the time. Instead I have vomit in my hair and I haven't gone to the bathroom alone in three years." She rolls her eyes and pulls at her sticky hair. "Jeffy! Stop biting your sister! I'm sorry. I have to go 'not spank my kid' before he draws blood again."

A young gothic looking girl with black lipstick looks miserable, "I hate life and I love to watch people writhe in agony. I wish I could be on the Doubt & Chaos Team. I would be so much more ruthless than any of those lightweights. How great was it when Jade turned out to be played by a guy? I almost actually smiled. Sucks to be you, Matthew. Now you are a gay." She smirks smugly.

Daniel chimes back in, "We actually had to search pretty hard to find people who weren't inspired by Matthew, but there they are, all four of them.

What we have noticed in overwhelming numbers is the amount of people who have been inspired by this adventure. People are going out of their ways to be kind to one another. Without knowing it Matthew has pioneered a worldwide call to action to love your neighbor as yourself. By his example the people have seen first hand what it means to struggle and still be compassionate. They have seen what it takes to stand fearless in the face of evil and not be crushed. This common man has proven to be a hero to many. Let's here from some of the many lives that have been changed."

A young man stops from doing construction to talk to the camera, "I was raised believing that hard work was to be looked down upon. People who did labor jobs were less than somehow. If they had only studied more and applied themselves they could have good jobs that pay more. I watched the transformation in Matthew's life. I watched how happy he became once he started working with his hands. It created a hunger inside of me to know that kind of satisfaction. At first I started working with a friend of mine on weekends doing odd jobs. I have loved it so much that I have started my own remodeling company. I finally quit my job two months ago. I love being able to create with my hands. I love helping people fix their homes. I love making dreams become a reality. I wish more people could experience the joy of hard work."

A weathered looking middle-aged man smiles big at the camera, "6 months sober today. After 35 years of addiction I have finally gotten clean. Better late than never. I was owned by that stuff for so long." His eyes fill with tears, "It is so nice to see life with fresh eyes. I have hope for the first time in my life. Sure I'm tempted all the time to relapse. When I am, I remember how Matthew has been tempted and what that means.

Giving in to your temptations doesn't make the pain go away. One is too many and a thousand is never enough. There is nothing for me at the end of that road. You are only tempted so you can be mocked and exposed for your sins. So I try to stay strong just a little longer, because I know it will pass. I see myself differently now. I want to be a hero too. I want to be someone people can look up to. I want to be an inspiration to someone who has no hope."

A man in his 30's confesses, "I'm ashamed to admit this, but from the time I was very young I have had problems with pornography and with lust. I have mostly seen women as sex objects. I cared very little about my wife's needs emotionally or otherwise. I would work hard so that I could pay to keep a wife so that I could have sex with her whenever I wanted to. If she wasn't in the mood I would become angry and would act out. I didn't really care about what she was feeling.

After watching the Jade sequence I felt like I saw behind the curtain of deception to some degree. Everyone knows that Venomous Itch produces pornography. We all pretend not to know his work, but it is so obvious. When the season began I actually spent quite a bit of time on the Internet admiring his endless library of smut. At some point it became disgusting to me. And my own behavior became disgusting to me. I realized that I didn't want to support this type of thing any more. I didn't want to be any part of it.

I feel like I have had to completely rewire my brain. I threw out everything I knew and started from scratch. It had gotten to the point where I was having erectile dysfunction with my own wife. My brain didn't respond to real women any more, only to pornography. This was so troubling to me.

At first I would blame her or my work or my diet, but it was my own fault. I was a prisoner and I couldn't see a way to escape. I'm not there yet. I am working on loving my wife more and treating her like a queen. It turns out my best friend was right here next to me the whole time. I was such a fool. Watching Matthew and Lacey work through their struggles has helped us to be honest with each other and begin healing from years of bad habits."

The camera widens out to reveal that the man's wife has been sitting next to him while he confesses this. She has been holding his hand. She speaks up, "My husband isn't the only guilty one here. I would use sex as a bargaining chip to get what I wanted from him. I would play games with him. I would also flirt with other men to get what I wanted from them. I would show more skin and wear revealing clothing on purpose because I enjoyed the attention I would get.

I don't think it was a conscious thing but I saw my husband as a meal ticket. If I could just be pretty and sexy enough he would buy me what I wanted. He took care of me financially and I let that be enough. Sure we 'loved' each other by the world's standards, but we didn't really. It is painful to hear these words out loud, but we both knew it for years. There was a cold war going on inside our home. We resented each other. We fought more often than we didn't. We almost got divorced more times than I can count. I think we mostly stayed together for the kids.

When Shane came to me and decided to be honest and vulnerable about his addiction to pornography I didn't know how to react at first. I responded badly. I blamed him for all our problems. I had pretended to not know for a long time, but I tolerated it because that is just how guys are and I didn't want to be alone. I filed for divorce and we separated for about six weeks. After talking to some of my friends and hearing their stories I decided to be honest with myself. This wasn't all his fault. I had played my part as well and I needed to own that and make it right.

So here we are two broken people trying to make it work against the odds. We are far from perfect. I know this, I love my husband now more than ever and I know he loves me. He has chosen me and I have chosen him and we are committed to each other no matter what happens."

A radio DJ finishes a promo and turns to the camera, "I'm Lil' Mike Johnson. I have been known as a shock jock for decades. Every day I would search for the most disturbing stories and content I could find and then I would share them with my audience. I had great ratings. I made good money. I had a huge following. I basically would talk about whatever amused me. It was an empty life. From the outside it might have seemed fun, but inside I was wasting away. I had lost faith in humanity. I saw myself as the clown that kept people laughing while the ship sunk around us.

At first I watched the show for research and show prep since everyone was talking about it. As time passed the true beauty of what was happening hit me. Anyone who can't see the spiritual parallels of The Hard Road must be blind. Here you have a man, a seemingly ordinary and anonymous man, going about his life alone and unappreciated. He starts to question his purpose when he is presented with the truth. He didn't realize how fully it was the truth at the time, but the truth to the best of his knowledge.

He then starts paying attention to the signs around him. He prays. He listens. He sees answers. He then starts to want more. He is no longer satisfied with the life he had before. He had lived in fear before. He didn't realize he was afraid, but he was. He was afraid of poverty. He was afraid of failure. He believed the lie that he was alone and everything depended on him. When he finally admitted he was lost and needed help his real life finally began.

But one prayer wasn't the end of the story. It was only the beginning. Once he started putting his faith into practice he started seeing real results. He saw real challenges too. But every step of the way he is being guided to a glory unspeakable that he can't even comprehend. What an inspiring picture of what God is doing for each one of us.

It wasn't long before I started to ask these same questions that he was asking about my own life. At first I asked the audience just to get their opinions and have some interaction on the show, but I was finally forced to ask myself if I was willing to continue on my current trajectory just because I had spent a lot of time getting here. As I looked ahead at the direction my life was going I didn't like what I saw.

I decided to make some changes. They were small at first. I didn't tell anyone what I was doing. I finally got the courage to let the cat out of the bag on the air. I expected to be mocked and receive a lot of pushback since I had a nasty reputation and there was a certain expectation from my broadcasts. The station manager took me into his office to discuss some concerns he had. I thought I was going to lose my job. I thought about it and I resolved in my heart to stand my ground and turn over a new leaf. I sat down and braced myself for the inevitable.

To my surprise, management was happy with the new direction of the show. Listeners had been calling in and emailing their support. There were countless people who told the station how their own lives had been changed for the better. They got on board and encouraged me to take it farther. It really felt good for all of us to be making a positive impact on our community. We started doing fundraisers for various charities. We devoted time every day for good news and uplifting stories. We probably have ten good stories for every one bad story right now. We are trying to get that down to absolute zero. We don't want to give negativity a place to flourish so we don't devote much airtime to it.

It has felt so good to be able to be a shining light instead of a sarcastic clown. I feel like there is hope and I will tell the world about what I have experienced every chance I get."

A housewife is looking down and she looks up at the camera, "I am ashamed to say this but I have been planning to end my life for quite some time now.

I have small children so I have been trying to find reasons to live for them. They don't deserve to grow up without a mother. I think of my husband and how it would affect him if I killed myself. I think of my family and my friends. I'll be honest it wasn't enough to make me want to live. Most days I couldn't lift my head to fake a smile. I was becoming more depressed by the day. I fantasized about how I would do it. I would think how nice it would be to leave this world and all the problems that came with it. I didn't want to feel that way. I just couldn't get myself out of this funk I was in.

Early in the season Ed Hastings came up to Matthew and admitted that he was going to kill himself that night. Those words struck me to the depths of my soul. You see I was planning on killing myself that night too. I saw the hope in his eyes. I saw how much Matthew cared about him when he cried alone in the car after he left. I saw Matthew taking steps to better his life. I decided I would at least try to live one more day and make the most of it. I could always kill myself tomorrow if I still felt the same way.

I heard some great advice. If you are depressed go find someone who has it worse than you and go be the friend to them that you wish someone would be to you. You will see that your life isn't that bad. You will also gain a friend and inspire someone. When Evan told Matthew that it was impossible to help your brother across the river and not get there yourself I took that as a personal challenge. I wanted to get across this river of depression so I made it my life's one last mission to test this theory. I didn't really want my life to end. I just wanted the pain to end. If there was any hope at all I wanted to reach for it.

Long story short I found a friend that really needed help. I offered to help her with her problem and she broke down crying almost immediately. She has become one of my best friends. I am so glad we have conquered this together. With each passing day it seemed like a small stone was taken out of my own heart as I helped her until finally I could lift my head up with dignity again. I waited months before I told anyone about my plans for suicide. I had a bottle of pills waiting with my name on them. Last week I threw them away. I don't want to end my life any more. I truly want to live! That is the first time I have said this out loud. It feels good. It's so true. I want to live my life to the fullest." She wipes tears from her eyes and looks off camera. Her husband comes and hugs her.

Dr. Edward Chapman, an anthropologist, starts speaking, "What we are experiencing is a worldwide phenomenon. It is one thing to talk about faith, but it is another thing entirely to see faith boldly demonstrated in the face of absolute despair. The world has now seen it and the world is changing for the better. Crime rates are at an all time low. Families are reconciling and setting aside their differences. Races are coming together in unity. Marriages are being healed. Suicide rates have dropped to less than half of what they were at this time last year. Drug use has slowed drastically.

And the ripples from this one event will ripple on throughout history. We are all witness to a new era that is being rewritten as we all watch with eyes and hearts wide open. There will come a time that we will look back and realize that the atrocities that had become commonplace have quickly faded and were replaced with faith, hope and love. Love not just in word, but in deed as well. It will be as if someone finally turned on a light switch."

Zeke comes back onto the screen with excitement, "A lot of people don't realize this but an anonymous donor paid for this entire show. He invested ten billion dollars of his own money to make it happen. He doesn't want his name or face to be shown, but when I spoke with him I was inspired to do the show. He is a man of few words. He simply said 'Zeke, I believe in the goodness of humanity, but it has gotten off track. People have thrown their hands in the air and given up. Everyone complains, but nobody has a solution. I want to find a man, one good man and challenge him in front of the whole world. If I can do that and he can stand the test then there might be hope for humanity again.'

He then told me the concept and I fell in love with it. As time has passed it has been an honor to be a part of his vision and watch it unfold. When I asked him about his investment he simply replied, 'I am giving everything I have for this. I am holding nothing back. If it works it will be worth every penny. If it fails then I suppose we are all lost beyond repair. How can I not try with everything that I am and everything that I have? There is nothing more important in life than this one thing. It is my life's mission to leave the world a better place than it was when I got here. This is my gift to the world'

I wish I could tell you about this man because he is so inspirational. He has such wisdom. He takes responsibility for problems that he had nothing to do with causing. He is willing to get his hands dirty and do the hard work. In fact, you would never know he was the owner if you did see him. Many of you have and you just passed him by as if he was nobody. You couldn't be more wrong. He is the living incarnation of greatness. We should all aspire to achieve such heights through humble service.

All right. I have talked enough. How many of you guys would like to see how Matthew is handling this new development in his life?" (The crowd goes crazy. It is a shout that is heard across the world.) Zeke pauses to soak up the moment. He closes his eyes, takes a deep breath and smiles. "Then let's get back in there. God speed Matthew. The world is cheering you on hoping to be right there with you as you cross the finish line. Stay strong brother."

11 Reflections

Matthew is sitting in a swing in an empty park looking at the ground contemplating his life. He has removed himself from as many distractions as he possibly can. He is doing some deep soul searching. He is asking himself some very hard questions. He doesn't want anyone from this world he lives in to influence what he does moving forward. In lieu of the recent news the judges have decreed one hour of silence from both teams to let Matthew gather his thoughts and move forward in the game. Matthew notices the silence of it all around him and in his head.

Matthew begins talking to himself as the world listens eagerly to what he has to say. "I have to decide what I am going to do next. If what I just heard is true than my entire life is a lie. I have been played like a pawn in a chess game. I have been a fool. I have stumbled blindly through a maze while people point and laugh at me.

It does kind of make sense. There have been so many coincidences in my life. I just started to believe that was the new normal. I stopped questioning it. But did they really have my best interest at heart? I don't know. Is my life just amusement for the masses? That was some crazy stuff earlier today. Two guys came and blew my mind and then stepped in front of cars to die and no one said a thing about it. That is highly unusual. Did I just imagine that? It didn't feel like a dream. I'm not on drugs. I don't know how to make sense of all this. I'm really confused. I'm afraid that the moment I ask for a sign my life will be filled with them again and the chaos will continue.

So while I am still in the calm before the storm I need to make some decisions. OK. The way I see it there are several options of what is happening. One. That guy Tom is telling the truth. I really am in a game and there is a team of everyday angels that are guiding me down a path that will lead to a huge prize. If this is true than I should keep looking and listening and try my best to do the next right thing. If this is true than I should let nothing stop me.

Honestly, I would have done it for free. I have had such joy since I have decided to change my life. As I look back even the bad things in my life have been for my good eventually. If I hadn't been beaten and pistol-whipped by thugs I wouldn't have met Lacey. If Evan's house hadn't burned down I wouldn't have had the opportunity to partner with him and make as much money as I did.

If I hadn't had the challenges I have had I also wouldn't have the experience and the wisdom and the blessings and the strength that come from conquering those things. Not to mention all the valuable life lessons I have learned. And I have had a peace in my life beyond anything I have ever experienced before. I have really loved being a blessing to people that have less than me. It has given my life meaning. And I am happy, genuinely happy.

OK. Second option. Let's assume Tom was telling the truth and Zeke was telling the truth. If this is true than I am disqualified and my game is over already. I might as well give up and ride the clock according to him. I will just wake up from this dream at some point and it won't have mattered anyway. I can go back to the life I had before as a loser.

If I were to follow that logic I could do literally anything I want with no consequence. I could treat people selfishly. I could use women. I could abuse drugs and alcohol. I could cheat people. I could eat anything I wanted. I could be lazy and worthless. After all, what difference does anything I do make at this point?

I just don't know how any of that would give me any real pleasure though. It is such a miserable empty life. I don't enjoy treating people badly. I don't enjoy being intoxicated. I hate feeling guilty. I hate the feeling of failing. And how many people would fall with me because I fell? If the world really is watching then they would watch me fall and if they had any hope at all it may be crushed by my lack of faith. I don't want that. I want to be an inspiration to people not a stumbling block.

OK. Option 3. What if none of it is true? What if I was just seeing things? What if I hallucinated or had a waking dream? What if I am delusional or insane? What if I think more highly of myself than I should? What if I am just a shmuck trudging through life's mundaneness and trying to invent an adventure that doesn't exist? So what if I am? Does it matter? If I am just a nobody that doesn't matter than I want to make the very best of this life that I can. And I want to make the lives of the shmucks around me the best that they can be while I'm at it. I want to make the world a better place for as long as I can. And when I can't possibly do it any longer than I will hold on just a little bit more. And as I sink slowly into the next life I will die knowing that I have done my very best. I want to die with dignity. I want to die with honor. I am not a coward. I will not shrink back.

That prize money would have been amazing though, wouldn't it? That is a lot of money. One billion dollars! One thousand million dollars! I can't even imagine what I would have done with that kind of money. I could buy an island and declare it my own country. I would have diplomatic immunity and be able to do anything I want because I would be above the law. No. That would be lame.

I could buy an island and have a beautiful exclusive resort with all kinds of cool things to do. I could have the best of everything. I could travel the world. I could have businesses in any field I choose. I could use my fame to write a book, a best seller. I could buy a yacht and a helicopter. I could buy a fleet of helicopters. I could buy a spaceship. I have a lot of options. But none of those sound very fulfilling.

If I were to be honest I just want Lacey by my side to enjoy life with. I love helping people. It seems stupid to work if I have that much money. Why go through the hassle of owning a bunch of things that I would have to maintain and upkeep? It seems like a waste of life. The more you own, the more it really owns you. So what should I do with the money if I actually do win it?"

He thinks deeply. He searches his soul. He tries to draw from everything he has ever known. "It seems like more of a burden than a blessing to have that much money. I don't know what I would do. I'll tell you what would be cool is to go find all the people that had been good to me throughout my life. I could make a list. I would go and find them and befriend them. I could eventually ask about their hopes and dreams as I worked beside them.

I would ask what made their hearts sing. I would listen closely and then give it to them. No. I wouldn't want them to know it was me. I would secretly arrange for their dreams to conveniently come to life for them. Then I would have the satisfaction of knowing that a good person was blessed. There are so many undeserving people that have money. It would be nice to have someone who actually deserved it be blessed. Really that is a selfish use of my money because I would be blessed more than they would. I would really enjoy that. Yes. That would be a life worth living.

I could become an undercover angel. I could go around finding people who deserved blessings and then be that blessing for them. I would have enough that I could do that for the rest of my life. Wouldn't that be nice? What a full life that would be.

You know, I don't have to have a billion dollars to do that. I can do that right where I am. It is easy to be incognito when you don't actually have anything. I can still help people with what I have now. I can start where I am with what I have with the people right in front of me. I think I am going to do that. No matter what happens I want to do that. I really enjoy making the world a better place. I love encouraging people.

Wouldn't it be nice just to hear God tell me what I needed to do? Wouldn't it be nice if he just came and sat right here beside me and put his arm around me and said ' Matthew, I love you. Here is what you are doing right. I'm proud of you. Here is what you are doing wrong. Fix it. Here is what I need you to do next. I'll guide you. Don't be afraid. I'll always be right here next to you.' That would be so nice.

But of course that won't happen. Which is fine I suppose. I know that God loves me. I know He is here beside me. Whether the game is real or not, God is real beyond the game. I know He is guiding me and I think I know what I need to do. I need to start by setting some things straight. I need to make a list of people I have wronged and make it right. I need to make a list of people that have wronged me and go and forgive them. I need to actually tell them that I forgive them so they don't have to carry that heavy burden with them any longer.

When someone is doing well I need to encourage them so they don't stop. I need to lift up the broken hearted. I need to hug the lonely and cry with them. I need to rejoice with those that are rejoicing. I need to show respect to people. Respect is a quality that is sadly lacking these days. I will live for an audience of one. Regardless of what the truth is I have decided to do what I believe is the right thing. And I feel really good about it."

Matthew stands up as he says this and although he doesn't know it the world stands up with him. There is something called the year of Jubilee in the Old Testament. Every fifty years everyone is supposed to forgive everyone else's debts. It is an opportunity for a clean slate. To start over new is such an incredible blessing. The fear is that you will forgive but the other person won't. This was of no concern to Matthew because he had finally experienced true freedom, freedom from guilt and shame and the threats of loss of money or status or possessions. None of it held any power over him any more. A heavy burden had been lifted from his heart. He felt lighter and he felt happy and content. His mind was made up.

His hour of solitude was also up. And now he was open to outside influence again. Doubt & Chaos wasted no time. They had been watching as all their hard work and their best-laid plans were laid to waste and they were furious about it. They all bickered amongst themselves. Each one blamed the others for their failure. No one wanted to take responsibility but in reality they were all to blame. Every attack they made only ended up furthering Matthew's game. It was so obvious to everyone but them.

FrienZee had hoped to throw off Matthew's game by telling him the truth but instead it has led him to decide on his own to accomplish his last three good deeds. Perhaps there was a bigger game being played where even what was meant for evil became used by good. Perhaps just as Matthew suspected God was working through all of this the whole time.

As Matthew was leaving the park a businessman walked up to Matthew with direction and purpose. "Matthew Jacobs. It is time. Your game is over. You can go home now." He pulls out a gun and aims it at him. Matthew doesn't resist. He closes his eyes and smiles. He raises his hands to Heaven and says, "I have been waiting for this moment. I want you to know how very grateful I am to have had this experience. I have thoroughly enjoyed every moment. I am even grateful for the hard times. I am sorry to anyone I have done wrong. Please forgive me. And to anyone who has done me wrong just know that I forgive you. I don't hold anything against you. You can take me now. I am ready."

The man lowers the gun and hands it to Matthew, "No, you have to do it. Those are the rules. The safety is off. Just put it in your mouth and pull the trigger. You will wake up on the other side. You are famous now. There is a party waiting for you."

"No, I don't want to kill myself. Thank you very much." Matthew says frankly.

The man is frustrated, "Take the gun. Finish your game. Go home already. It is over."

"Oh wait. This is a temptation. You can't actually do anything to me, can you? You are powerless over me. You can try to get me to do it, but you can't actually make me do anything without my consent. I can tell by the look in your eyes that I am right." Matthew says as he starts to walk past the man.

The man is furious, "Then we will bring down wrath upon you! We will make your life miserable. You will be met with plagues and pestilence and pain and torment. With every breath you take you will be you begging for it to be your last. You have made a grievous error."

"I suppose you could be right. If I am to be punished I would rather it was for doing the right thing. I suppose when we are told we have to take up our cross we forget that at the end of that road we will be mocked and beaten and killed. If that is to be my fate then so be it." Matthew says as he walks away.

The man throws the gun at the back of Matthew's head but as he does Matthew walks in front of a stop sign. The gun bounces off the sign and misses Matthew. The man is fuming and cursing as Matthew walks away.

A girl walks in front of him on the street and he notices her shirt. It says, "The world needs more men like you." She stays in view just long enough to read the shirt and then she walks out of sight. Matthew looks up at the sky and smiles. A tear wells up in his eye. He doesn't even question it. He knows he is on the right path. He goes home quickly.

As he walks in the door Lacey is there waiting for him. She doesn't say anything. Neither does Matthew. They just hold each other for a very long time. Finally Matthew kisses her and says, "I love you so much. I am so glad you are in my life. You are such a blessing to me. I don't deserve you."

Lacey chokes back tears, "Are you kidding me? I'm so proud of you. I don't deserve you. I love you more than love!"

Matthew looks her in the eyes and says, " I need to ask your forgiveness."

"For what?" Lacey asks.

"For the whole Jade thing first of all. I don't know what I was thinking. It must have been very difficult for you. And I am starting to have some fuzzy memories. I don't think I was the best husband to you. I think I neglected you and put work first a lot. That was wrong of me and I ask that you forgive me for it." Matthew says with regret.

Lacey hugs him tightly, "It was hard. Thank you for acknowledging that. I have had many years of loneliness while you were on the road. I tried to be a good wife to you. I felt that if I could just be better than maybe it would be enough for you, but I never was enough."

"So, I'm a monster? I'm so sorry. I don't remember that. I will do my best from here on out to be the best man I can be and to always make you feel loved. So, will you forgive me? It is important for me to make this right with you." Matthew says.

"Of course I forgive you. I love you. I can't think of anyone I would rather spend my life with. I am so proud of you. You are my hero. Will you forgive me?" Lacey says with a satisfied smile.

"There is nothing to forgive. I don't want to hold on to pain any more. It feels good to let it all go. Is there anything you would like me to do to make it right between us?" Matthew asks.

Lacey thinks for a moment, "No. You have already done so much more than I could have ever asked for. Your changed behavior is more than enough for me."

Matthew pauses, "There is another thing. I think I messed up my game somehow."

Lacey tries to pretend to not know what he is talking about, "What game is that, Hon?"

Matthew tilts his head, "Ok. I understand if you can't acknowledge what I'm saying. I'm going to just say it anyway. I think our lives are about to get very difficult and I think it is my fault. So no matter what happens just know I am going to stay true to my convictions and I love you very much."

Lacey looks into Matthew's eyes like she wants to say something, "Hmm? That is, interesting. Well, of course I don't have any idea what you are talking about. But hypothetically speaking if what you are saying is true than just know that I support your decision. I will always be by your side and I love you too. Very much."

"This is going to be hard isn't it? Should I be scared?" Matthew asks.

"I wouldn't be if I were you. The light inside you is so much stronger than any darkness you will ever encounter. Don't worry. You were made for such a time as this. I suppose if any of us knew what a difference we made in the course of history we would be able to stand up to anything. Stay true Matthew. That's all you have to do. Stay on course. Don't be distracted by what you see or hear. You are on your way to vic..." Lacey stops herself, "...to good things. You are on your way good things happening."

"Why did you stop yourself?" Matthew looks intently at her, "Oh, you can't say, can you? Ok. I won't be afraid. If you say so then I will trust you. If you see me afraid please put your hand on my shoulder and let me know you are still there with me so I can stand under the pressure." Matthew says bravely.

Lacey looks down, "I can't promise that. It isn't my call." She reaches in a drawer, "Wear this ring and know that I am there with you no matter what comes your way. Just think of me and know beyond a shadow of a doubt that you are always on my heart. I will defend you every chance I get."

"Is this my wedding ring? It fits perfectly." Matthew asks.

Lacey smiles, "It's just a symbol of my eternal love for you."

12 Make it Right

The next morning Matthew woke up early and started to make a series of lists. He tried to remember everyone in his life that he had hurt and he wrote their names down. He also wrote what he had done to hurt each one of them. He made another list of people who had hurt him. He tried to recall as much of his life as he could. He tried to retrace his path through life and see where pain may have gotten him off course. Not just the initial shock of being hurt, but the choice to continue carrying the pain and stay a victim and a slave to these hurts. He wanted to make peace with everyone as much as was humanly possible.

He started to reflect on his life starting from his childhood. He probably could have been a better son. He was a selfish child. He wore his parents out and he knew it. He would push them to the end of their limits most days. His mother had died of cancer when he was a young man. He never fully processed that pain or what it meant to lose a parent. His father had been a rock in his life, but Matthew had never really told him how much that meant to him. His father had sacrificed so much of his own life to make sure that Matthew had everything he needed. He was such a great man. Why hadn't Matthew ever thanked him?

He had bullied his little brother Peter. He took advantage of his size and would terrorize him often. He publicly humiliated Peter for his love of computers and technology. He didn't encourage his gifts. Peter was smarter than Matthew and Matthew knew that. There was part of him that felt jealous. Matthew had been his parent's life until Peter came along. Peter got away with so many things that Matthew never would have. It was petty holding on to this resentment.

He cheated in school sometimes. He shouldn't have done that. He was difficult with teachers that were giving the best years of their lives to make sure he had the tools he needed to succeed in life. There was a substitute teacher that he had been particularly mean to named Mr. Hazelwood. He was quirky and shy. Matthew had taken advantage of him by exposing his insecurities. After that Mr. Hazelwood had quit teaching. Matthew felt partly responsible for that. He wished he could make it right.

He hadn't been a good friend to his childhood friend Noah. They used to hang out all the time, but as the years passed he had let the busyness of life be an excuse to not spend time with him. He missed his friend. He should reach out and make time for him.

There were so many shortcomings in his life the more he thought about it. It was almost overwhelming. He was determined to see this through. It was important to him.

He thought about girlfriends that he had when he was younger. He could have been better to them for sure. One particular girl named Emily came to mind. He has in college at the time that they went out. They loved each other very much. He was one year older and so he graduated before she did. He acted like they would stay together and he would wait for her.

He graduated and never saw her again. He never broke up with her. He just stopped answering calls and he never called her back. He could tell from her voicemails that she was very hurt by this. There was no good reason for doing this to her. She was a beautiful girl. It was cruel. He was scared and believed lies. When you are young small amounts of time seem like forever. He hadn't thought about her in many years. He felt real remorse for the way he had treated her. He resolved himself to apologize to her.

He had worked alongside a guy for a few years early in his career named Sean. The two of them did the same job and they both did it well. Many times there was limited work in their specialized field. One of the two would get the job and the other one wouldn't work. Matthew felt that Sean was better at his job and he knew more.

At some point he was tempted to attack Sean's character to potential clients so that they would choose him instead. The things that he said were loosely based on the truth but they were personal and they were very hurtful. It did irreparable damage to Sean's reputation. Eventually he was forced to move away from the area to get work. Sean probably didn't even know that it was Matthew's fault. That didn't really matter. He needed to make it right somehow and seek forgiveness.

Shortly after that Matthew had a very difficult client. She wouldn't wear clothes that were easy to put a microphone on. She refused to stay on the stage. She mumbled and wouldn't use her microphone properly. She would stand in all the places that he told her not to stand. She was very rude to all of her staff. She was impossible to please.

She would change her mind all the time but then blame whoever was standing closest to her at the time. Everyone knew it was her fault but she was a ruthless boss. Everyone that worked for her was anxious all the time. Her name was Kim. He did a tour with her for six months. He had seen how she acted and he didn't like it at all so he wrote a scathing article to people in his industry laying out all of her imperfections.

She probably never even knew or cared. She probably didn't remember him. He still felt a need to somehow make peace. He shouldn't have slandered her name. It wasn't right. No matter what she had done he should have been better than that.

He free-lanced for a company several times over the years called Aquarius. More than once he felt that they shorted him on his checks. They would argue and justify their actions. He told them he had let it go, but he felt he should level the playing field and take matters into his own hands. He started the habit of padding his hours when they weren't paying attention. He "accidentally" took things of value home with him. His attitude on those jobs left a lot to be desired. At the time he felt good about doing all those things, but looking back he was really robbing them. There may be ramifications, but he wanted to be honest. He wrote the owner's name on his list. The owner's name was Scott.

Matthew had a friend for years named Nick. One day Nick borrowed five thousand dollars from him because he was in a bad place in life. Nick promised he would pay Matthew back. Matthew knew he was in a bind and was happy to help. After a few weeks Nick stopped answering Matthew's phone calls. He wouldn't answer emails or texts. He unfriended Matthew on social media. He talked bad about Matthew to his friends. And eventually Matthew stopped trying to reach out to him.

Matthew knew he probably wouldn't get his money back when he loaned it to Nick. He was fine with it. He just wanted to help. He was just calling to hang out. They had been good friends. It hurt Matthew to lose a friend more than it did to lose the money. He wanted to restore that friendship and make sure Nick knew he was forgiven of the debt. So he put Nick's name on his list of people to forgive.

Matthew had another friend named Allen. Allen gossiped a lot. He had a real problem. He couldn't keep his mouth shut. He couldn't keep a secret. He talked about everyone's problems to everyone else. Matthew tolerated it because he liked Allen. Matthew had started going out with a girl and it was serious.

Allen also liked the same girl and so he started talking to her about her and Matthew's relationship. He let her vent to him. And then he started talking about all the reasons why she shouldn't stay with him. It seemed innocent at first. Allen may have even had good intentions. He was oblivious to his own problems. Those words, just like poison, drove a wedge between the girl and Matthew and shortly after that they broke up. Matthew blamed Allen and they stopped hanging out. He needed to forgive Allen.

While he was on the road many years before he paid for his meal with a credit card. The waitress stole his identity. It was several months before he even noticed the bogus charges on his credit card. She had racked up about ten thousand dollars in credit card debt in his name. She also bought several cell phone plans complete with phones and accessories in his name. She spared no expense. Years later he would still notice suspicious activity on his credit report. He went to apply for a home loan, but couldn't qualify because his credit score was too low. This confused him since he paid all of his bills.

He finally traced it all back to this one waitress, Tammy. He knew her name and address. He knew she had been in prison before on petty offenses. Because it was across state lines and it was difficult to prove he never bothered prosecuting her. He figured what comes around goes around. He hoped she would get hers for what she had done. Now, as he had a different perspective, he felt it was important to reach out to her and let her know that he forgave her for what she did to him.

Another time a celebrity speaker named Tom had called Matthew out by name from the stage. He called Matthew an idiot and said he didn't know what he was doing. The entire crowd looked at him in disgust. His crew sided with the celebrity since he was paying them. It tarnished his reputation. Matthew was upset so he spit in the presenter's coffee and gave it to him after his presentation. Tom continued to rail on Matthew while he sipped the coffee. Matthew just smiled to himself and said, "It is my financial pleasure to serve you."

This was a tricky one to resolve for Matthew. He wanted Tom to apologize for the way he acted, but he probably didn't even remember. And he wanted to apologize to Tom for spitting in his coffee, but Tom was known for being very litigious. He sued everyone for every little thing. He was a very petty person. Matthew decided he might have to forgive and forget this one without tipping his hand. He might just have to let this one go and avoid the fight that seemed inevitable.

A worker named Alex did a job for Matthew last year. They were both overworked and irritable at the time. Matthew felt he hadn't done a good job. Alex felt like Matthew was trying to get something for nothing. He had been unclear about his expectations and changed his mind without telling Alex. Tempers got heated. Alex swallowed his pride and finished the job even though Matthew had been difficult to work for. Matthew purposely wasn't there when Alex finished the job. And later refused to pay him for any of his work. The two spent tremendous amounts of energy trash talking each other to their peers, but the problem was never resolved. Matthew felt that he should pay his debt and make it right.

Suddenly this became the most pressing matter. Matthew stopped making the list and looked up Alex's phone number. He called him. Alex was shocked to hear from Matthew. He was hesitant at first, but he was curious. Matthew apologized for his part in the situation. He offered to pay the entire bill plus interest. Alex refused to take interest.

Alex was truly touched by this gesture and admitted that he really needed the money right now. Matthew paid him over the phone while they were talking. He asked for his forgiveness for the way he had acted and for the things he had said about Alex. He didn't go into detail about everything that was said. It was enough to just right the wrong. He didn't ask Alex for an apology. He didn't accuse him of any wrongdoing.

He simply owned up to his part and paid his debt. He apologized for waiting so long. Just before they hung up Alex said, "Hey Matthew. You didn't have to do this. I really appreciate it. It means a lot to me. I forgive you. Will you please forgive me as well? I could have handled that situation a lot better myself."

And so bridges were mended. Friendships were restored. Hurts were healed. One by one Matthew went down his list and made restitution for his sins. And he forgave those that had sinned against him. It wasn't nearly as hard as he thought it would be. He paid what he owed in money and in remorse. He forgave what was owed him. He made his own version of the year of Jubilee. He leveled the debt. He cleared the table. It felt really good to be free from it all. His heart was lighter.

Why had he waited so long to do this? Why did he want to harbor pain and bitterness for so many years? Why did he insist on keeping a collection of people he hated? Either way it was over now and he was happy. He had freed all the captives. In so doing he had also freed himself. He was ready to start fresh. This time he wouldn't let things go for so long. He determined in his heart to be an anti-crastinator.

13 Let The Trials Begin

While he is thinking this he hears a loud knock at the door. He answers the door and a delivery driver holding package says "Matthew Jacobs?" Matthew nods his head, "Yes."

"You have been served." The delivery driver hands him a manila envelope and starts to walk away.

Matthew is confused, "Wait. What is this?"

"Don't shoot the messenger. You have been summoned to court. You will stand trial today at noon. Look at the paperwork." The driver walks around the corner and goes out of sight.

Matthew opens the envelope and sure enough he has been summoned to stand trial at noon today. It is unclear what his crime is or what the court case is judging. But in no uncertain terms it demands his presence. He reaches for his phone. "Searching for signal" with a spinning wheel. He looks around. All the streets are empty. He looks at his watch. It is 11am. He has one hour to prepare his defense for unknown crimes.

He begins to panic. This is what the guy with the gun had been talking about the night before. My trials are about to begin he thought. He looked at his phone again. Still no signal. This was frustrating. He hadn't even showered this morning. His hair was a mess. He was standing in the street in his pajamas. He decided to take a shower and change. He felt this would be the last time he had peace for a long time. So he went inside and got himself ready.

Once he was ready he looked at his watch again. It was 11:35. He still had no cell phone signal. Which meant his GPS wouldn't work either. He stepped outside again. Still empty streets. No cars. No people. He didn't recognize the address on the summons. He closed his eyes and asked for guidance. While his eyes are still closed he hears a car pull up. It stops right in front of him. The passenger window rolls down. "Get in. You are going to be late."

Matthew asks how this stranger knows where he is going. The driver doesn't even look at Matthew. He just says, "We don't have time for games Matthew. Get in."

Matthew gets in the car and the driver quickly gets them across town. He doesn't stop at stop signs or red lights. He drives very fast and comes to a screeching halt in front of the courthouse. "Hurry, they are waiting for you." Matthew is in a daze. He gets out of the car and walks into the courthouse. He braces himself as he walks in, "So, this is how my story ends?" he mumbles to himself as he goes through security.

The courthouse is filled with human arrows that just point him in the next right direction until he is led into the courtroom. The courtroom is completely filled with people. They all stand up and turn around and look at him as he enters. They stare as he walks down the center aisle towards the judges' bench. He is in a daze as he walks through the crowd. They all seem to know who he is. The whole thing is very surreal. He is intercepted by a man in a suit who ushers for him to sit down in the defendant's chair. He whispers, "Matthew, I'm John. I'll be defending you. Don't say anything. Just let me do the talking."

As Matthew sits down the crowd also sits quickly. They are eager for what is next. A panel of judges walks in wearing black robes. There are twelve judges. They look vaguely familiar, but Matthew is so distracted that he doesn't really look at them. Once the room settles Zeke walks in and begins the trial.

"Matthew Jacobs. You are about to be judged. Are you ready?"

Matthew is nervous. John nods at him. Matthew says, "I'm so sorry. I'm very confused. I don't know what I'm being accused of sir." The crowd laughs.

Zeke points at Matthew, "This guy, huh? Don't you just love him?" The crowd applauds loudly. "Everything will be revealed in its proper time. Let's get started. Are you folks ready?" The crowd cheers and whistles and claps. "Ok folks, calm down. We need order in the courtroom so we are going to ask you to hold your applause until the final decree. I know it's hard, but please in the interest of time stop yourselves from making any noise. This will move the trial along. If you can't control yourselves security will escort you out. Are we clear?" The crowd is silent. "Perfect. We have an understanding. Now let's get started.

Matthew, at the beginning of the season I explained the rules of the game to you. I told you that you would be blindfolded but you had to walk a path set out before you. It was timed. You had to listen to your conscience who was tied to your fate as well. The crowd was given complete freedom to distract you from achieving your goal however they saw fit. Do you remember this happening?" Matthew nods.

"Well it's time to take off the blindfold and see how you did. Before we do that how do you think you did, Matthew?" John nods at Matthew to answer.

"I don't remember all the good deeds or the good things that could happen. At the time I didn't realize I would be living this game. I thought I was just working a show. Of course I want to think I did well. If I was being honest I think I fell short more often than not. I'm not really proud of myself. I have been afraid a lot. It has been a hard road. I don't think I completed the road. I think I probably strayed. But Zeke, can I just say something really quickly?"

"Yes, we want to hear from you." Zeke is eager to hear what Matthew has to say.

"I don't think I deserve any prize, but" he tries to hold back tears, "but I am so very grateful for this opportunity. I already feel like I have won. I have learned to appreciate my life. I have learned to love other people. I love helping them. I have learned to live by faith and not by sight. I have learned to forgive and how to be forgiven. I have learned what a privilege it is to work hard with your hands. And so no Zeke, no I don't think I finished this game and I don't think I would even know what to do with the prize money if I got it. But I have no regrets. And like I said I am so very grateful for what I have been through."

There isn't a dry eye in the audience. Zeke pauses and takes a deep breath. He opens his eyes wide and dabs the corners with a tissue. "Well, that certainly is an inspiring testimony. Let's find out if you are right. We are going to take this blindfold off slowly in increments so that you can see yourself as we saw you.

But first we would like you to see behind the curtain a little at the people who had your best interest at heart and those that didn't. I know this will be hard for you to see. This is the team of people who tried to keep you off the straight and narrow path. We know them as Doubt & Chaos. You will probably recognize them by the way they speak to you.

Sue Dough, MediaM, Venomous Itch, and FrienZee come out so Matthew can see you." They all walk out one by one and sit at the prosecutor's table. They barely make eye contact with Matthew. They whisper among themselves and look over from time to time.

Matthew thinks to himself, "This is it, huh? These are the people that have tormented me for the last year? They don't look like much. It was all smoke and mirrors. It was all a lie. Why did I let them bother me so much?"

Zeke continues, "And now for the still small voice that you heard every day. This is the team of everyday angels that were selected to be your conscience. Your enemies were strangers. They did not care about you. They only cared about the money and about winning. But this team, your team, loves you. They were hand picked to help you win this game Matthew. Are you ready to meet them?"

Matthew is very eager, "Well, yes I want to meet them. Are you kidding me? Before they come out I just want thank you whoever you are. I heard your voices and you gave me hope in the darkness. You did an amazing job of guiding me. If there were any problems I am sure they were my fault."

Zeke introduces his team one by one, "Let's see if you recognize any of these people. On defense and encouragement is your best friend since childhood Noah Tallman!" Noah runs out and hugs Matthew. Matthew is shocked and ecstatic. He doesn't know what to say. Noah finally sits down. "And on media and tech is a man that you call little brother, Peter Jacobs!" Matthew is stunned, "You are so smart! When did you grow up like this? I'm so proud of you. You look tired." They hug each other. Peter sighs, "I am tired brother. I'm exhausted. But it was worth it. You are worth it."

"And next on offense and exhortation we have the very man that gave you life in the first place, your father, David Jacobs!" David comes walking out slowly. Matthew can't hold back his tears. "Dad! I love you so much!" David walks up to Matthew. Matthew puts his hand out to shake his father's hand out of respect. David walks right by his extended hand and hugs Matthew's neck. He holds him tightly and pats his back. He kisses his forehead. He turns him around to the crowd and puts his arm around him, "This. Is. My. Son! And I couldn't be more proud of him!"

"And finally your conscience in the flesh. The one who stands beside you through all your victories and all your failures. Your bride. Your lifeline. Your support system. Lacey Jacobs, come out here!"

As she turns the corner Matthew can't believe how beautiful she is. He wonders what he has done to deserve someone like her. The courtroom is silent though the tension is thick. Outside the windows the streets are filled with people cheering as they watch this reunion.

It is so loud from the outside that you can't hear what Matthew and Lacey are saying to each other as they get closer. They hug sweetly and kiss each. The roar of the crowd gets even louder. The crowd in the courtroom looks like they are going to explode.

Zeke smiles and says over the PA, "Fine, you can cheer for them for one minute." The roar of the crowd is deafening. They are so happy for these two. Matthew is overwhelmed. Eventually Zeke quiets the crowd.

"Ok we have to get through this. We know you love these guys and I'm sure they appreciate your support. We have to keep going. Presenting for Doubt & Chaos is a Senator from Kentucky, Devon Petty. Before you ask he is no relation to Tom. I already asked. And representing the defendant you have already met John Josephs. So, now that you know the players let's get this trial started.

Oh yeah, you haven't met the judges yet. Let's get some lights up here. The creator of the show wanted to have judges that would have the absolute least chance of showing you any sympathy. Ex girlfriends, old bosses, people you had beef with, old teachers that you had driven crazy, people you had done wrong, people who did you wrong, basically anyone who didn't like you was put into a pool and we picked the ones most likely to hate you."

Matthew shakes his head. Under his breath he says, "Well, this should be interesting."

Zeke continues, "In a serendipitous twist of fate these were all the same people that you made lists about this morning before you got here. You have made an effort to reach out to them and seek reconciliation, but it will be interesting to see if they still hold onto the past grudges or if they let it all go and show impartiality. You are literally hoping for judges with no grudges.

We will hear more from them as we get deeper into this trial, but for now it is time to present your cases. We will start with the prosecution. Devon, you have the floor."

Devon stands up and buttons his jacket, "Thank you Zeke. I will remind the judges that my clients didn't have to make Matthew do any bad thing. That was never their goal. If it had been they would have succeeded in that too. Their only mission to win the prize money was to stop Matthew in whatever way they saw fit from completing his ten good deeds and collecting his ten good rewards within the one year time constraint. I believe that they have completed this task and I'm sure once I present evidence you will agree with me." He sits down. Doubt & Chaos huddle up and whisper to each other as they look over at Matthew.

John Josephs stands up and looks at the judges and then he turns around and looks at the crowd. "Ladies and gentleman it is undeniable that Matthew Jacobs and his team have complete the hard road victoriously. We can go through one by one, item by item if it pleases the court, but the defense doesn't think it is necessary to laboriously dredge up the past when the evidence is so overwhelmingly in the defense's favor. It seems like beating a dead horse."

The judges huddle and whisper as they hold their hands over their microphones. After quick deliberations one of them looks at Devon, "Would the prosecution like to forfeit?"

Devon stands up, "No, your honor. We agree with Matthew that he doesn't deserve the money. We wish to explore every step and we believe that when we do you will see that we are the rightful prize winners."

The judge replies, "Very well, as you wish. Prosecution may call their first witness."

Devon begins, "The prosecution calls Daniel Codey, the statistician."

Daniel walks up to the witness stand. He is sworn in. It is made clear that he is the same man who does statistics for the show. He confirms. Devon then asks him to read all the good deeds, which he does,

1) Inspire someone who has lost hope
2) Help an enemy
3) Give away something that is precious to you
4) Turn the other cheek
5) Love the unlovely
6) Be a friend to someone who desperately needs your friendship
7) Volunteer and expect nothing in return
8) Forgive the one who has hurt you the worst
9) Ask forgiveness from the ones you have hurt the worst and then do whatever it takes to make it right with them.

10) Give away everything you have

"Will you please tell the court in detail how Matthew has completed each of these?" Devon asks

Daniel is happy to go through the list, "Absolutely. The first good deed was to inspire someone who had lost hope. Matthew did this when he refused drugs and he inspired Ed. Ed had intentions of killing himself that night, but was inspired. Since then Matthew has inspired countless people that had lost hope. If I were to exhaustively go through this list it would take the rest of my life.

The second good deed was to help an enemy. He did this when he helped Sharon, the homeless girl who broke into Evan's flip house. He helped her to reunite with her family after her and her son had ruined all his hard work. Since then Matthew has helped countless people both friend and foe. He is generous with his time and his money.

The third good deed was to give away something that was precious to him, which he did when he gave his money to Evan to save him from financial ruin. He was only required to give his time, but instead he gave $150,000 of his own money.

The fourth good deed was to turn the other cheek, which he did in the alley when Stephen was being mugged. He stepped in front of a gun. He was punched and he didn't resist. He offered himself in Stephen's place. He was then pistol-whipped. Technically that would have been enough but he was willing to die for a total stranger even though he was given every opportunity to leave. Matthew has made a habit of turning the other cheek in every aspect of his life. It is now a lifestyle.

The fifth good deed was to love the unlovely, which he did with Stephen. What greater love is there than to lay down one's life? This requires no further explanation.

The sixth good deed was to be a friend to someone who desperately needed his friendship. He fulfilled this objective when he came to Lacey's aid and left Jade behind. She was desperate and needed a friend and he was a friend to her. Since then Matthew has been a friend to many people.

The seventh good deed was to volunteer and expect nothing in return, which he did at the homeless shelter. This is not debatable.

The eighth good deed was to forgive the one that hurt him the worst. He completed this objective at gunpoint in the park. He freely forgave everyone who had done him wrong. He didn't stop there he also compiled a list and made sure to contact the people on that list and let them know that he forgave them. Some of those same people are on the judge's bench as we speak.

The ninth good deed was to ask forgiveness from those he had hurt and make restitution. As I just described he completed that objective far beyond what we required by the rules.

The tenth and final good deed was to give away everything he had. Matthew has actually done this on several occasions. When he was willing to give his life more than once he was literally giving away everything he had including his existence. He also openly confessed and I quote 'I don't think I deserve any prize'. He didn't say this with any expectations. He literally was willing to give away a billion dollars without a fight. And he was grateful for the opportunity."

Devon interrupts, "We completely agree with Matthew. We don't think he deserves the prize either. We have already said that. The prosecution doesn't believe that Matthew actually gave away everything he had. He was willing to, we agree. But intention is not the same as action. This is the first reason that we believe that the defense has failed.

Now if you will please tell the court the ten good awards and tell us when he claimed each one?"

Daniel replies, "I would be happy to. First was to learn a new trade that he loved. He did this with Evan and house flipping. Second was to be healthy. His health was a direct result of the hard work he did and immediately followed his completion of the second good deed.

Third was to be physically fit which was also a direct result of continued hard work. This followed his completion of the third good deed. Fourth was to defeat his demons, which he did with Jade. Fifth was to find the love of his life, his wife Lacey. Sixth was to live at peace. We feel this is so painfully obvious that it requires no further explanation.

Seventh was to be healed from a long-term ailment. The ailment was his loneliness. It was healed when he came back to Lacey. Eighth was to experience true freedom. He has had true freedom for quite some time. The most noteworthy has been when he recently forgave all the people that he held grudges against.

Ninth was to change the world for the better. We believe that not only has Matthew Jacobs changed this world for the better but he has made an everlasting impact on the real world as well, one that will ripple throughout eternity. And finally his last prize is to win the lottery. And once you finish this charade he will do just that."

Doubt & Chaos murmur amongst themselves. Devon responds, "The prosecution has several problems with your responses. Particularly prizes seven through ten. We don't believe that loneliness counts as a long-term ailment. We don't believe that he has experienced true freedom since he is still in a medically induced coma hooked to machines for life support. We don't believe he has changed the world for the better. And he hasn't won the lottery. He never even bought a ticket."

John Josephs stands up, "Objection your honor. Does he actually have a question for the witness or is he just projecting his own opinion?"

"Sustained. Do you have a question for the witness?" one of the judges asks.

Devon is calm, "No further questions. The defense may cross-examine"

John Josephs stands up, "The defense has no questions for this witness your honor."

Devon stands back up, "The prosecution calls Sue Dough to the witness stand."

"Objection."

"Sustained. Mr. Petty, Sue is not a witness. She is clearly part of the team that would benefit from Mr. Jacobs' loss. Everything she said would be unfairly biased. No one on either team will be allowed to testify. You have played your game. We have all witnessed your game play. We admire and respect it. We thank you for your service. Does the prosecution have any witnesses besides the opposing team members?" one of the judges asks.

Devon looks at the team questioningly. They shrug and shake their heads. He straightens some papers and looks down. He looks at his notes. He slowly crosses off his list. He bites his lip and sighs. "No, your honor. I suppose we don't have any other witnesses. The prosecution rests."

One of the audience members says sarcastically under his breath, "Pretty strong argument."

The judge looks sternly at the guy who has said this, but then ignores him. "The defense may call their first witness."

John stands up slightly, "The defense rests your honor."

The judge looks confused, "The defense rests? The defense hasn't even begun. Are you sure?"

John stands up, "If it pleases the court. We could call witnesses from around the world to verify what we have all seen, but we believe that Matthew's testimony stands alone with no need of defense. It is painfully obvious to everyone that Matthew has completed the course ahead of time and well beyond all expectations. He has been an inspiration to the world, your honor. If he doesn't deserve the money, then who does?

This brave man has pioneered a way through an often difficult and treacherous journey through faith. He had no assurance of reward nor did he even desire it once he was made aware of the possibility. In fact, after thinking through the possibilities he settled in his heart to use it to help other people that he felt deserved it. He has no selfish ambition. He has no malice. He loves unconditionally. He will use this money to make the world a better place.

And quite frankly I fear for the world if these monsters win a billion dollars. Who even knows what kind of evil they will be responsible for creating if they are allowed to go unchecked? That being said the defense doesn't wish to exhaust the court's time. We simply ask that when you judge this game and this man that you use the same good heart that we know you all aspire to. And as I said before the defense rests."

"Very well. You have been heard. Does the prosecution have any final statements?" The judge asks Devon.

Devon looks nervous, "Yes, your honor. As I stated before the prosecution doesn't feel that Matthew completed the course to our satisfaction. That alone should be enough. Doubt & Chaos is an elite team of professionals that should be taken seriously and respected. They want the prize money. And they deserve it too. They have worked hard for it. They have overcome a lot of obstacles themselves.

Do you know how hard it is to make a good man do bad things? He is impossible to break. We tried everything we could, but he just kept listening to his conscience and ignored us most of the time. He just wouldn't take our bait. It wasn't fair to us. We feel that if he would have bitten on even one of our temptations than it could have snow balled into a huge victory for our team. One thing would have led to another and his path would have ended up being much different. We would like a retrial"

"Is there anything you would like to add before the judges deliberate?"

Devon is defeated, "No. I have said too much already. I would like my last statement to be stricken from the record."

"Well that's not how it works. You don't get to strike your own statement from the record. But if it makes you happy I don't think it will make any difference. Consider it stricken." A judge says mostly out of pity.

The judges all stand up and walk to their chambers one by one. The crowd stands up out of respect. Once the last judge has left the door closes. Zeke comes back up to the front of the room.

14 The End of the Road

"The judges are going to deliberate now. We don't know how long this will take. Deliberations can go on for hours or even days sometimes." Before he can even finish his statement the door opens back up and the judges walk towards their seats. The crowd stands again. The judges sit down. The head judge addresses Matthew directly.

"Matthew Jacobs please rise to hear our verdict just as you have risen to this list of tasks. Please stand here in the center so we can all see you. Thank you. Before we give our final judgment is there anything else you would like to say?"

"Yes. I am sorry. I am sorry I waited until this morning to make things right with all of you. Not because you are my judges, but because it was wrong of me to harbor that resentment for so long. It hurt our relationships and I feel like we all missed out on a much fuller life.

Also I'm sorry that I wasn't a better person. I feel like I could have done so much more if I had only known sooner what I know now. I don't deserve any money. You don't have to give it to me. I am far from perfect. I am determined to live the rest of my life with purpose. I will live it to the fullest. I vow to all of you that I will be a better man than I have been.

And in case this is the last chance I have to speak I just wanted to say one more time how very grateful I am for this opportunity. My memory is starting to come back slowly and I remember wanting to play this game. But as it turns out I needed to play this game. The amount of time and energy and money you have all spent on me to help me learn what I was so desperately lacking is humbling to say the least. So thank you again. I feel honored to have been a part of all of this."

The head judge speaks frankly to Matthew; "I find it amazing how completely oblivious people are to their own behavior. I am constantly shocked at this phenomenon. In the Bible Jesus talks about the final judgment. He separates the people like sheep from goats. It is that clear to him. To the goats he says when I was hungry you did not feed me. When I was thirsty you gave me nothing to drink. When I was sick and in prison you didn't come visit me. The goats are stunned by this statement. They question him. When did we see you hungry, thirsty, sick or in prison and not help you they ask.

He says whenever you didn't do this for one of the least of these you didn't do it for me. Jesus had disguised himself as all of the unlovely people because what good is a person if they are only good when they think there is a reward for doing so? Yet they made excuses. They tried to blame others. They implied that if they knew they would have acted differently. All the while they were oblivious to the fact that they were truly rotten people."

Matthew hangs his head, " I understand." He starts to walk back to his seat.

The judge yells after him, "Please let me finish. Then Jesus looks at the sheep and says come into your glory because when I was hungry you fed me. When I was thirsty you gave me something to drink. When I was in prison you visited me. And they are equally as oblivious to their own actions. They say when lord did we see you hungry or thirsty or sick or in prison and help you? He replies whenever you have done these things for the least of these you have done it to me.

Matthew Jacobs you are a sheep, my friend. You have faced your demons and defeated them all. You have walked by faith. You have loved fearlessly. You have given yourself freely to anyone who needed you. You ask nothing in return. And you are grateful for the changes, the very hard changes that you have had to endure. You have inspired the world. You have shown us a real life example of what a man should be. We are forever in your debt. Now come into your glory. You are a truly good person. It is my honor to tell you that after a forty seven second deliberation the judges decided unanimously in your favor. You have walked the hard road and you have completed it. Congratulations!"

And the world cheered loudly, as so they should when goodness prevails.

Light is not the opposite of darkness. It is the absence of it. Let your light shine. Take it to all the dark places and test this theory. Live victoriously. I'll stand with God, even if I stand alone.

Made in the USA
Monee, IL
15 April 2023

31923914R00100